Death is an Illusion

L Lee Kane

TSL Publications

First published in Great Britain in 2020
By TSL Publications, Rickmansworth

ISBN / 978-1-913294-68-7

Dedication

For Robin C Kane
And a long life together

373 BC

The couple floated through the morning mist like ghosts, silent and eerie in an intricately carved boat that arched gracefully on bow and stern, crowned with carved dragons, teeth bared menacingly. Its eyes pierced the water, gliding quietly to the wayward side of their homeland.

"We must flee, husband, before the earth swallows us whole. The land is shaking, and I fear for our lives."

"Hurry, Muri," Shira whispered to his wife. "I can hear the thunder of the ocean as it crashes on the beach. The wind roars like an angry beast. We must run or we will be engulfed before we can retrieve the clay pot. We must retrieve the pot...we must..."

They passed no fewer than several boat lengths of a stone image of the Crete invaders—every face arrogant and masterful—world-conquering imperialists. The latter came to destroy Helike and make the citizens their slaves.

They hurriedly beached their small craft. "Look, the sky is darkening!" Muri screamed.

"Where are you two going? Get back here." The stern-faced slave master cracked his wicked hide-whip onto the backs of frightened men trying to escape.

"Don't look back! Run," Shira yelled.

The crack of the stout thong resounded in the air. A black cloud appeared, covering the face of the sun. It spread rapidly to the horizon. The ground heaved in rolling tremors that lasted only minutes. Still, it seemed like forever, throwing men and women into the air and down into the depths of the earth.

"It's almost too late," Muri cried out.

The ground swelled, and the land broke apart to the rim of the volcano as they scrambled to a hidden grotto protected from all sides of view.

Inside the grotto, the couple dug with speed, and from a sealed clay pot, they brought out a codex with coordinates that pointed to a new land and carried it away with the golden mykite that would keep their people alive. Husband and wife fled the interior of the cave just as high waves, infuriated and maddened by some tremendous force, swept over the tall cliffs and crashed across the feet of the gigantic structure of their Warrior God, Ares. The light of the day went out. The night of the total eclipse had come. A massive black pall covered the vault of the heavens; strange rains of blood-red water and white ash mingled and cascaded onto the causeways and covered the dome of the temple of their ancestors, before the war between the islands.

Below, Shira and Muri hurriedly ran from the caves. At the same time, their brethren threw down their tools, heeding not the whip and curses of their masters, who themselves scrambled up the side of the mountain to the safety of the caves in the nearby hillside.

A huge tidal wave with tremendous force swept over the mighty statues that had just been hoisted to a platform to be set up. The land shuddered, and eerie darkness crept over the area, as if it was the last day of earth.

Terrified, the slaves ran away but were swept back by the raging force of a hundred tsunamis. Cracks in the earth overtook the men and women fleeing for their lives on this terrible night. The mighty ocean had toppled the island from her foundation deep, deep into the depths of the sea, and the heaving waters now covered a whole massive land where life had at one time been a paradise of the people of the kingdom of Helike.

Carrying the clay pot and a bag of mykite, a golden mushroom that grows in caves, husband and wife raced down the mountainside to their people's massive ships that lay hidden in a cove. Behind them torrential rainfall, exploding fires, flaunted the collapse of their homeland.

The remaining survivors huddled, waiting for the earthquake to abate. They watched as their temples, homes, and crops disappeared. Many of their ships crashed into the roiling, muddy sea and were swallowed by the ocean. Nearly all the people had been engulfed by the catastrophe. The few islanders who survived were destitute, no tools, no clothing, no shelter, no food, and little land. Around them hissed and seethed the boiling waters that rushed into the fiery pit. Above, dense clouds of steam, smoke, and ash cut off the light, making impenetrable darkness.

The despairing cries of their friends and comrades who perished in chaos still rang in the ears of the survivors.

The next morning, the sun finally broke through the veil of clouds, and looked down on the scene, the remaining islanders clung to one another, motionless, reason gone, and stared with unseeing eyes where once was a vast island.

The islanders who survived the earthquake boarded the only remaining ship in the cove and sailed, using the stars to navigate, to a land far away where they could settle.

These were the people who landed and inhabited Italy. It was a tropical country with valleys and plains covered with rich grazing grasses, while the low grounds were shaded by luxuriant growths of tropical vegetation. Mountain ranges from the bowels of the earth stretched themselves through this paradise.

Many did not like the customs of this new land and dreamed of sailing to an area where they could begin anew.

Shira and Muri boarded one of these massive ships, and set sail for a new land with opportunities, taking with them their map of a new world and their mykite.

January 15, 2020

Luci walked up the ramp to board an Air France flight back to the United States. Many unresolved issues had left her feeling anxious and terrified of the future. It had been a long journey, from the death of her parents to traveling to Europe in search of the last codex written by Jesus Christ and avoiding The Order. She was exhausted and settled down deep in her seat and waited for the seatbelt sign to go off. She felt the thrust of the engine as they exploded into the air and was pushed hard against her seat.

One day, she thought, she would have so much to tell her child about the strength of his grandparents who guarded the secrets of the lost Cathars. As the jet leveled off, the seatbelt sign was extinguished, and that was her cue.

She got up to stretch her legs, heading to the washroom to freshen herself. Since her first month of pregnancy, she seemed to have to go to the restroom every hour. Upon her return, she saw a puzzling piece of paper left on her seat. The note was written with scrawled handwriting and a cryptic message. She glanced at her neighbor, sitting next to her on the aisle, but he was fast asleep.

She sat back down and stretched her arm, reaching for her bag to retrieve her glasses and pulled the paper out of the envelope:

"I've stumbled upon an ancient piece of pottery with a codex inside telling of the location of a lost city in South America that grows a mushroom that has curative powers. Someone is killing those who know."

Luci gazed around once again. Everyone was watching the onboard movie, reading a book, or talking to one another.

Luci glanced sideways, wondering who had left the message. The young man across the aisle sat rigid in a suit and snored into his starched shirt. The middle-aged lady beside her stared out of the window, sadness etched her face as she clutched a grubby tissue. Luci wanted to speak with her but said nothing because sorrow, fired by a desire for solitude, made people crawl inside themselves. Luci's own grief of her many losses was always tucked deep inside.

She reached into her backpack and drew out a travel-pouch of pocket-sized tissues. In a gentle gesture, she tucked the packet into the lady's palm. They exchanged a glance, and Luci nodded in understanding

Luci settled back in her seat. An abrupt mixture of smells wafted down the aisle. The aroma of coffee and tea made her nauseous. She covered herself with a blanket and fell into a deep sleep.

Startled awake when the cabin lights came on, Luci sat upright and pushed her tray table forward. People shuffled to the lavatory while the airline hostesses brought coffee down the aisle. Luci couldn't wait to see the skyline of San Francisco, Coit Tower, and the Trans America Pyramid. It had been a long journey that left her unsettled. She was carrying Max's child, a baby conceived in love and cherished above all else. She had wanted to tell him at Charles de Gaulle airport before her flight took off, although, as things stood, he might never know, his job had interfered in their lives once again.

Luci glanced down into her bag, pulled out her cell phone and threw her head back against the seat.

@lucidefoix u will die 2nite

Who in the hell sent this text? Everything was done, ended. They had found the codex, retrieved the text for the Cathars, and The Brotherhood of the Order was either dead or in jail.

Blood pumped in Luci's ears. Her heart fluttered in her chest like a hooked fish wriggling to break free. She glanced out of the window at the passing runway buildings and tried not to think about the warning.

Luci sensed something lay in hiding, waiting for just the right moment to attack.

***

At last, the plane shuddered to a halt outside the terminal. Most of the passengers jumped up, not waiting for the seatbelt light to go off. Chatter erupted as people fought to grab their bags from the overhead bin. Standing up out of her seat, Luci swallowed hard and tried to forget the text and the knot in her stomach.

The man from a few seats back bumped into her and mumbled an apology. Although his eyes beamed warmth, they also signaled something dangerous.

Luci reached up to the compartment to lift out her bags but, because of her height, had difficulty reaching her case, which had been jostled to the back of the bin.

The same stranger fell against her again. "I'm so sorry. Please let me hand you your bag, that's the least I can do for roughing you up twice."

"Thank you, I'd appreciate that." Luci gave him a quick once-over. He was handsome: blond hair, light blue eyes with deep frown lines. He had the lived-in look of someone comfortable with himself and his abilities. His body showed none of life's pleasures; it could have been carved by Michelangelo. Toned and athletic.

She took a step forward. Faded china-blue eyes, as she now thought of him, did the same.

From the corner of her eye, Luci watched him stand his ground as someone jostled him and shoved him forward, tumbling into her once more. "Ah, sorry," he muttered. "I think we need to quit meeting up like this."

Meeting like what? she wanted to say but instead said nothing. Could he be the one who left the note on her seat?

She pulled her coat closed against the morning mist off the ocean, and she trudged down the stairs toward the terminal, glancing at her cell phone again. On the screen was a photo of her and Max in France. His arm was around her, and her face glowed with contentment and hope. It tore out her heart that he stayed behind for his next mission with the government.

Luci tapped a number into her cell and waited, hoping Max would answer.

Her other hand still clutched the crumpled note. Keeping it hidden from prying eyes, she looked it over once again and wondered what secret could be so deadly. She balled up the note and stuffed it into her bag.

What's the ancient secret?

***

Grabbing her bags, she hurried out of the terminal. Luci stood on the curb and hailed a taxi to take her to the Marriott hotel a few minutes away. Before entering, her thoughts went back to the note. "What type of writing on that pottery could carry information on curative medicine?" She shivered, although not from the cold off the San Francisco Bay.

The atrium in the hotel was like a breath of fresh air; it was open. Tall glass windows faced a striking view of the San Francisco skyline.

At the check-in counter, a welcoming concierge provided her with a room and key. Luci trudged toward the elevator doors but hesitated as she spotted a familiar looking man. She was too tired to try and place the face.

Up the elevator, she traveled to the third floor. She glanced at the sign for directions to her room: fourth door down on the right. She slipped the key and heard it catch. Kicking the door open, she was astounded; the concierge wasn't kidding, she had a beautiful view, and it was convenient to the pool.

Luci unpacked a few of her belongings, including a swimsuit She was determined to go for a swim before she slept. It always relaxed her muscles after a long flight. The comfy robe provided by the hotel made her sigh contentedly.

The note's words still lingered in the back of her mind, a stalker lurking in the shadow. "*Someone is killing those who are looking!*"

***

She slipped out of the room and opted to take the stairs to stretch her legs. The indoor pool was dark, very inviting, almost womb-like. Luci slowly stepped down into warm water, staying motion-less for a while, she luxuriated in the peace and quiet of the moment.

She swam laps in the American crawl, slowly at first, then she picked up speed. Luci slapped her arms down hard in the water, every stroke was her anger and frustration at Max's sudden depar-ture and lack of explanation. Exhausted, she rolled over with her ears just below the surface and floated around the pool in peace.

Suddenly she was jolted out of her reverie; someone's hands were on her body, hands grabbed her hair and yanked her under the water. Breathing was her primary concern; she managed to force her way to the surface, sucking in a quick breath before she was pushed back under.

She had to stop this from happening. Soon she would be out of breath. Her ears were assaulted with a deep rumble of the cascading waterfall at the opposite end of the pool and she couldn't touch bottom.

She grabbed at the boulders. Big ones. Their soaked profiles protruded from the surge. She pawed at the water to get away from the person steering her toward a sharp rock. She kept her arms extended, leading the way, and feeling until her hands slammed into something hard.

She didn't bounce off of it. Instead, she held tight, trying to catch her breath. Her head emerged.

"This is only the beginning, Luci." The stranger slipped away into the darkness.

Water thundered past her shoulders, she held fast to the rock to get her mind together. Thankfully, she wasn't being held down any longer. The sudden feeling of a panic attack, and ice cold fear, was coming on.

She sucked in several deep breaths, shook the blur from her eyes, and saw she was alone again. Breathe, Luci, slow yourself down.

A poolside young man rushed toward her with towels in his hand. "Are you okay?"

"I'm not sure. I've got this awful cramping, and I'm having trouble breathing. Did you see what happened?"

"I saw a man climb out of the pool. He rushed past me as I was coming in. Did he hurt you?"

"He certainly tried. Oh my God, oww!" Luci howled. "Something's wrong, please call an ambulance, I'm pregnant and, oh my God, hurry."

He picked up his cell phone, called the reception desk, and asked for an ambulance. He eased Luci out of the water and threw some towels on top of her.

Luci was bleeding from her head and from between her legs. She was shaking and thought she was going into shock.

The pool boy threw a blanket on top of her. "Is there anyone in the hotel I can call for you?"

"No," she said. Then everything went black.

January 21, 2020

Monterey State University

Luci left the hospital with only a few days left to prepare for her class on the Cathars. Rummaging around her desk for a pen, she thought, if anyone thinks a college campus is a haven for academic pursuit, fellowship, and civility, they haven't been paying attention for the last twenty years.

***

"Devon, I just asked you a question about the Cathars and Pope Innocent III. Can you please share with the class exactly what you were discussing?" Luci demanded.

Devon turned a bright red and sank deep into his classroom seat. "I said you were hot, had long legs, and electric hazel-green eyes." The class erupted in laughter.

"Sorry, I must not have heard you correctly. Could you please tell the class how me being hot has anything to do with the Cathars?"

"Sorry, Professor de Foix, it won't happen again."

The bell rang, shrilly announcing the end of the period. Everyone jumped up and crowded out the door.

Someone entered the classroom. "Hey there."

Turning, Luci saw that it was her adopted sister Sarah. "Hey there, right back at you. What are you doing here?" Luci said with surprise. "I thought you were in Crete."

"I was, but there have been some rumblings regarding a lost race of people with an advanced society and a two-thousand-year-old document that's linked in some way to information that Nick received regarding a lost civilization that sailed from an island near Crete to South America. Want to know more?"

"I think I've had enough adventure for a lifetime, so thanks, but no thanks, I'm not traveling anywhere soon."

"I told Nick you'd say that. That's why he asked me to come here personally and show you some of the artifacts that have to be found," Sarah said.

Changing the subject, Luci said, "Someone left a note on my seat on the airplane. It mentioned something about a secret document, a lost city, and magical potions. It also said people were dying to get the information."

"Could be connected. Why don't you take a look?"

"Well, sure, I'd be happy to look at things from right here. Where are they?" Luci asked, hesitantly.

"In my backpack in the rental car. But first, I think we should catch up with things that have been happening in our lives."

"You mean you want to know how I'm doing after Max and being attacked at the hotel."

"For starters, but let's do it over dinner."

"Why don't you go to my home and get comfortable, take a shower, just relax, and I'll be there after my kung fu lessons."

"You started that up again?"

"After the attack, I thought it would be wise. I have no idea what that guy wanted or why I was attacked, but I'll be damned if I'm at least a little more prepared," Luci said.

"I can understand that, and I'm so sorry I wasn't there, and I'm sorry about the baby Luci," Sarah said.

"I wish you had been there, Sarah, I lost something that was made by Max and me. Something I can never get back. I've lost so much, I don't think I can take much more."

"I'm so sorry, Luci," Sarah said, grasping her hands.

"No one could have known, but I don't think it's over. I've had a feeling I'm being watched."

"Under the circumstances, I can understand that. Why would anyone be coming after you, though?"

"Unresolved issues?"

Sarah smiled. "Well, whose heart have you broken?"

"Not anyone I'm dating, maybe from the discovery of the codex."

"That's over with. Everyone is gone or dead."

"Not Janet."

"She survived, huh? I doubt she attacked you or is following you."

"Maybe I'm paranoid, but I have been getting text messages, and they are making me jumpy."

"You didn't tell me that," Sarah said, alarmed.

"That's why the kung fu."

"I want you to know how sorry I was leaving you. I owed my father to get him Solomon's lost seal."

"What you owed me was the truth about who your father was."

"I know. I hope you'll forgive me one day."

"The important thing is that he's dead and Solomon's ring is buried deep inside the Vatican where no one can get at it. I'm also sorry your father died because of it. We need to continue this talk, mend fences, and clear the air, Sarah."

"I know that, but I never meant to do you any harm. You have to believe me on that."

"I do believe you. You're my sister, and we've been through a lot together."

"Okay, go to your kung fu class. You kick ass while I go to your home. We can meet up later."

***

@lucidefoix I didn't know you had such a pretty sister. Sliced and diced.

***

Time spent on the punching bag was well worth the expended energy. Luci looked forward to a shower and dinner with Sarah and picking up the pieces of their once close relationship. Taking up her bag, she wiped a towel over her face and looked out the window of the kung fu studio. The same car that had been parked next to her at the college had followed her here. It wasn't a coincidence, she was sure of that.

Carefully, she leaned over and picked up her coin sword used in tournaments by Taoist monks. In ancient times it was considered to be a magical sword that warded off evil. She walked outside the studio door, sword in hand.

The windows of the Mercedes were blackened so she couldn't get a look at the driver. Walking toward the door, she reached to knock on the window. The car reversed and exploded out of the parking space, hitting a car before speeding away.

Her sifu, or instructor, ran out. "Who was that, Luci?"

"I have no idea. That's what I was trying to find out."

"You really shouldn't be carrying that sword outside of the studio. He was probably just interested in the classes, and now you scared off a potential client."

"I doubt that. He followed me from the college and has been sitting in that car for over an hour, waiting and watching."

"Let's get back inside and practise your Wing Chung," Sifu said, looking worried.

Luci smiled, opening the door for her sifu. He walked in a little nervously.

***

"How was the workout?" Sarah asked when Luci arrived home.

"Fine, but after a quick shower, let's get something to eat."

"I've been on an underwater exploration but had a break. Nick called me regarding a document written by a Catholic priest who had traveled with Pizarro to Peru in search of new land to claim and gold to discover. He thought you might need a change of scenery, and possibly another adventure using your talents in archeology as opposed to teaching. Besides, it will be fun to get away together."

"I'm not done at Monterey State until June. I'd be happy to check it out after."

"I told Nick, but he insists you come back with me. He said it was important. Besides, it's almost Christmas break. It will be great to get away, see your family."

A rumbling came from her coat pocket—her cell on vibrate. "Wait a minute, Sarah." Looking down, she saw it was from Max.

They had met on the campus at Monterey State University two years before. They later teamed up to discover the Last Cathar codex that members of a Catholic Order had coveted. They were all lucky to survive, and she certainly didn't want to start this craziness all over again. Looking at the text sent chills down her spine. *Meet me in Crete.*

"Who is it?" asked Sarah.

"It's Max. He sent a text; he wants to meet."

"Does it say anything else?"

"He's still with the CIA."

"Oh God, not that again."

"I'm not ready to see him. I wouldn't know what to say or where to begin."

"Sure, you do. Just be honest. Changing the subject, I've been on this job in the South Seas for the last three months. I received a text from one of the scientists onboard the ship. He asked me to take you back to Crete. I had told him about you and your ability as a philologist."

"Another text, I seem to be pretty popular. What's up with that?" Luci's phone beeped again.

@lucidefoix hell waiting 4 u 2 nite. U will enjoy what I do to you.

Luci felt a tingling in her spine and a wave of nausea. *What did this mean? Who was doing this?*—*were these text messages and the man in the pool connected somehow? Why does everyone want me to go to Crete?*

"Are you okay? You've turned white. What does that text say?"

"Yes, I'm fine. It's just about school, that's all." So much had happened between Sarah and her in the past, she wasn't quite ready to open up to her yet.

"Then this could be good for you. Hey, I'm just a messenger, I'll show you some of the pottery we found at the site, and the information that Nick sent. You judge if it's worth taking a short trip to check an archeological dig."

"Okay, but I'll need to process all of this, Sarah," she said, turning over the shard Sarah had given to her.

"I'll be leaving for Greece in a few days. You have time to think about it. Anyway, and this is why I came...I need you to translate the writing on this shard we found in Crete. It could lead us to the exact location of Helike where other shards were located," Sarah said, pointing to the shard on the table. "The island sank, and it's only because the waters are receding that we can now see some of what was once a beautiful city. Plato spoke of it often, believing it was Atlantis. It would be so helpful to me, for us, to stay in contact with this expedition. I don't know what we're heading into, but from what I hear, the Russians are gearing up with their own team of scientists. They don't know the old languages and pottery like you do. We can crack this together."

"Let me get my purse. I'll leave Max a message letting him know where I'm going, I think."

"I wouldn't say this to you, Luci, if I didn't love you, but you really need to do something in the field you were trained for."

"I began the process of starting up my own archeological company. I've even rented a building in downtown Pacific Grove. What do you think?" Luci questioned.

"It's something you were trained to do, so I'm in." Sarah smiled.

"Okay, partner, what would you like to name our company?" Luci grinned.

"Let's get something to eat. We'll talk about it over a bottle of champagne. Text Max if you want after."

"Thank you, Sarah. Just give me a few minutes, and I'll be ready."

***

Where would you like to go for dinner? It's about seven o'clock: Fishwife, Fandango, or McDonald's, and we are talking until you give in and go with me."

"I'm in the mood for local, so how about Fishwife?"

"Sounds good, Luci. What else is going on? You seem on edge."

"Someone on Facebook said 'think of a five-letter word that describes you.' All I could think was angry. I'm tired of death, tired of being afraid, sick to death of the climate in the academic world where people get away with murder, and I'm so angry at losing people I love."

"You haven't lost me, Luci. You never will," Sarah said, tenderly.

"I know, and I thank you for being there for me. Hey, I've just thought of a name for our company. How about the Natural Scientific Archeological Agency."

"That was fast, but I like it. It sounds very professional."

"I've really been thinking about this for a long time. You just gave me the right push to help make it happen."

"Can we go eat now? I'm starving."

"Me, too.

***

Sarah and Luci opened the door. Something whooshed past their heads and lodged in the doorframe. Luci spun around. An arrow from a spear gun loomed at eye level. What the heck was going on?

"What the fuck was that?" Sarah screamed.

"Get back in the house. We need to pack and go now."

***

As Luci crammed her clothes into her suitcase, Sarah called every airline to find the first flight to Greece. A Virgin Air flight was leaving from the San Jose airport at 10 p.m. No time for food, they locked the front door, ran to Luci's gray SUV in the garage, and screeched out of the driveway heading for the freeway.

For the hundredth time, Luci looked down at her phone while Sarah drove. Putting on her glasses, she stroked the cell's screen, hoping to see a message from Max. "Dammit."

The phone beeped. For a moment, she squeezed her eyes tight, wishing away any threat.

The phone beeped again. Luci sagged into her chair like a rag doll. A shiver crept its way up her spine, and her stomach tied itself in knots.

***

@lucidefoix missed u, u r leaving 2 soon, but u won't get away. U R a dead woman.

***

Luci read her latest phone message but ignored the constant beeping. Too many nuts, waiting for an opportunity. Maybe it was a good idea to get away for a while, help Sarah with her underwater project...Or perhaps it wasn't underwater, only hidden.

Sarah picked up Luci's phone and read the message, then placed it down on the chair while they were waiting for their flight. "Luci, hey, this is bad, have you contacted the authorities?"

Luci looked at Sarah.

"That bad?"

"I've learned a whole new set of dirty words from this guy, and the authorities aren't interested."

Sarah glanced at a woman in a tight pair of jeans, with rips around the knees. "I'd give anything to look like that."

"Maybe she works out every day and doesn't immediately stick her nose into a computer when she gets up in the morning."

"Point taken. She probably doesn't eat dessert every night, either."

"Probably not. I do know why people wear holey jeans. They can slip the bottom of the stem of the wine glass between the tears and have their hands free to eat." Luci giggled at that.

Sarah smiled, seeing Luci lighten up a little. "We need to discuss what I've been hired to do on the expedition and why Nick needs you. Let me get the pottery for you. Thought you might enjoy studying the pictures of it while we're flying."

Their flight was announced.

"Let's board, and we can talk at length."

"Before or after the food? Virgin Air has a great menu and lots of desserts."

"Okay, you had me at dessert. Let's go."

***

"What flight are they taking, Xander?" Ivan asked, gazing out at the water at his home in Crete.

"I managed to gently persuade Luci and Sarah to leave Pacific Grove. They're on Virgin Air to Greece."

"You need to be on that flight. No screw-ups this time, Xander." Ivan thought his counterpart resembled a string-bean, thin and gaunt like a marathon runner. "You should have already taken Sarah before she met up with Luci at the college. We need Sarah's tech skills with the LIDAR technology and the ROV (automatic submarine robot)."

"*Da*, I understand, sir. I will be on that flight, and we will get one or both of them as soon as they land."

Planning the murder of a loved one to convince each other of the necessity of helping to discover the Helike civilization, and if they were indeed the Atlantians like Plato believed, Ivan gazed out of his hotel room to watch the sea while scribbling notes, flipping back and forth between pages to check what he'd written. Beside him, Sergei stared over his shoulder.

January 22, 2020

Luci took out her iPad, opening the protective case that also served as a keyboard. The iPad was a better choice of computer when traveling. It was smaller for starters, and it had a long battery life which would last longer than a laptop if left in battery mode, but just in case, she had packed extra batteries.

"What do you know of the Helikes?" Luci asked.

"Not a lot, but what I'm interested in is how cultures of different nations influenced the civilizations of other countries," Sarah answered.

"What do you mean?"

"The Egyptians, the Phoenicians, and the Helikes all had pyramids, right?"

"Yes, so?"

"Tell me, how the Incans and the Aztecs had the technology and the tools to build their pyramids? Isn't it a little bit too coincidental?"

"It's a good question that I don't believe has ever been answered. Is it possible that the Helikes made it to South America and were able to actually influence the other cultures with their building and possibly their advanced ability in agriculture?"

"The discovery of Helike, with the information that Nick was able to find regarding the priest of another civilization at the same time as the Incas, is mind-boggling. Hints of this culture have been found in nearly every country: Ireland, Egypt, Scotland, Spain. This civilization might have been so advanced that discovery of them would redefine history as we know it today," Sarah said excitedly.

After the airline hostess delivered their food, they ate hungrily and drifted off to sleep.

Luci was startled awake by the announcement of their flight about to land. She nudged Sarah awake, and both prepared for their landing.

Before Sarah and Luci exited their flight, something prickled at Luci's neck. She jiggled her shoulders to stop the tingle taking control of her whole body.

Then it dawned on her. He was close by again, and now she wasn't imagining he was following her. She turned to adjust her suitcase on wheels as she exited the airport.

Sarah was up ahead, hailing a taxi. A large, black SUV pulled to the curb in front of her. Two men grabbed Sarah and dragged her in the side doors.

Forgetting the spy, Luci dropped her luggage, ran to the SUV, grabbing at the handles, frantically trying to hold on as they pulled away from the curb. "You can't take Sarah! Stop, you're making a mistake," she shouted.

The sheer speed knocked Luci's hands loose, and she fell to the ground, hitting her head on the pavement.

The airport police arrived and called for an ambulance. The EMTs checked Luci over, stabilized her neck, and eased her on a gurney that they slid into the back of the ambulance.

"*My sister, someone kidnapped my sister!*" Luci cried. "I have to find her."

"You're not going anywhere. Calm down now." The paramedic stuck her with a needle.

"What did you do? You don't understand…"

January 1536

It was bad enough they had to be secreted away from the people who lived on this land. Everyone was different here. They had a different language, and they were so backward from the civilization that her people had originally come from in Helike long ago. Her relatives had survived the hardship of the seas, traveling to Spain and then to Cuzco. Here they would make a new life in this godforsaken country. Other survivors from their lands were scattered across the many islands.

Calisto's father decided to move his people much further inland to create their own world. He would walk among them, trying to communicate, showing them how to build sound structures and to grow abundant crops of food, to no avail. The Inca people were afraid of her people and set out to harm them. They were superstitious and believed her family were white devils. The Incan villagers invaded their huts continuously, destroyed crops, slaughtered their goats, and killed many of her people.

Calisto slowly got up from her table and watched as the brown people came closer. She would have to move and move fast to warn the others. During the daytime, she stood as a protector like her father had once done to safeguard their community. Suddenly, a loud bang made Calisto jump.

She couldn't risk others coming to their hidden cavern. The location of the hollow would always need to be uppermost in her mind. She hid her daybook back in a clay pot in the undergrowth of the grotto and fled into the dense forest, looking for the hidden opening to the entrance where her people lived. She glanced behind, worried someone was following.

Behind her, a twig broke. She ran to the entrance of the cave and put wild brush in front to hide the secret opening; she didn't want anyone finding her people. She ran toward the opening then fled even further into the grotto that was surrounded by caves with many tunnels. Unwanted warriors who ventured into the tunnels became disoriented and lost. Many men had died to keep the New Helike's sacred valley a secret.

January 22, 2020

Luci called Nick from the hospital. Before he could get out the word *hello,* she shouted, "Sarah has been kidnapped. Two men in a black van took her. I've called her, and there's no answer."

"My God, Sarah's gone? The Russians are now in Crete. They're probably the ones who've taken her. They need her help to survey certain ocean locations with the ROV and the endoscopic cameras with scanners **to** recover more pottery shards. Sergei is helping the Geographic Adventure team discover more sites at Helike. He's gone missing as well. I don't want to frighten you, but this is far too coincidental. I think you need to take precautions. I'll call a friend to see if he can track down Sarah's kidnappers."

Luci jumped in. "I'm not leaving until we find her. I'm going back to the hotel and will wait to hear something. I remember what one of the men looked like. I know I've seen him somewhere before, I just don't know where. And I've also been receiving threatening text messages. They seem to know everywhere I am."

"Do you think they have a locator chip on your phone? How long has this been going on?"

"Since I flew from France to San Francisco, Nick." Changing topics, Luci said, "Sarah had been trying to reach you. Where have you been?"

"I've been searching the archives at the Vatican and found more documents from Andres Lopez dated 1600. He spoke of a golden mushroom with curative powers."

"This sounds very promising for future pharmaceutical cures for many of our modern-day ailments."

"He goes on to describe a large city, rich in gold, silver, and jewelry, located in the middle of the jungle of Cuzco. The archives also state that ancient people from Helike survived and eventually made their way across the oceans and settled there. Do you have any idea about the writing on the shard?"

"No, not yet. I was working on it on the plane."

"I've been doing some research myself and was about to fly to South America, specifically Lima, regarding the priest's discoveries."

"Why, Lima? I thought we were supposed to be finding information regarding Helike and the people who lived there," Luci asked.

"Yes, you are. But now we have to locate Sarah no matter what it takes. You decipher the pottery shards and then contact me. Then we can discuss where I've been and why."

"Did you know Max sent me a text message?"

"No, I didn't know, I need to contact him, I think he can help us find Sarah, he has the contacts and the necessary abilities."

***

Sitting in the hotel room was not getting Luci closer to finding Sarah, or answers about the Helikes for that matter. She picked up one of the pictures of the shards and noticed, not the writing but, what looked like a star constellation.

Luci wasn't familiar with astronomy, so she picked up her bag to head to the local library. When she was leaving the room, her cell phone vibrated. Looking down at the message, she silently screamed.

***

@lucidefoix don't go to the police. We have Sarah, and will cut her unless u do as we say. Go to Sontinio...we know you have the missing shard, we need you to decipher it.

January 1536

In her Mitera's (mother's) kitchen, Calisto lit a candle and carried it to the kitchen table. Next to the cloths sat a small, squat glass bottle she used for writing and painting her tablet. Placing the candle on the table, she winced as a drop of hot wax splashed onto her finger.

Calisto loved this room. It reminded her of her father. As the guardian of the cavern, her mother had moved them inside after a close call with the Incan people and had this home built. Calisto used to sit at her Mitera's feet and listen to her tell stories about their homeland of Helike, the people, the crops, and the curative powers of the golden mykite that lay hidden deep inside the caverns. Those tales had been written about and passed through the generations. They fired her imagination, filling her with a desire to heal people.

A few months before, her uncle had given her Mitera, whose birth name was Athena, a huge cooking area. Built from stone, it featured alcoves down the sides and wooden racks to store her clay pots. Metal and copper pans hung inside the hearth, where long-handled ladles were fastened to iron hooks in the ceiling. The cottage floor was cobbled with wood from their mighty sailing ships.

A few brushes lay drying beside the fire. Calisto hated plucking the hair from animals, so she used split palm leaves. Her Mitera had taught her to make her own ink by breaking up oak galls and mixing them with soot, wine, water, and gum arabic.

It hadn't taken long for her to write down the tales her Mitera had told her. She had worked late into the night burning candles. She kept it secreted from the people outside their village and strangers who ventured their way.

Her mother had drawn pictures inside her books of the herbs deep inside the caves where the water lay hidden. Beside each of her mother's drawings, Calisto wrote directions on the remedies and amounts needed to cure the descendants of the Helike people. Many unusual diseases affected her people in this new land. Still, the golden-colored mykite seemed to help ease the pain and suffering.

After today, she would continue to paint, but about the people of Helike and the herbs her mother grew and the curative mykite.

February 9, 2020

Luci made her way to the library to search out books regarding Helike from the earliest period. Much of her knowledge regarding the Helikes came from an old book she'd discovered, a journal handed down through the centuries. She gleaned as much information as she could regarding the survivors. From the information that Sarah had learned on her expedition, Luci understood that *Helike was an ancient Greek Poseidon city that disappeared in the winter of 373 BC. It was located in Achaea near the town of Boura, which, like Helike, was a member of the Achaean League.*

This bore quite a bit of similarity to the lost island of Atlantis. Luci wondered if this was a coincidence.

Both were centers for the worship of Poseidon, the Greek God of the sea. Plato described him in his journals as the "patron of Atlantis."

The submerged town has been one of the most significant targets for underwater archaeology. Numerous scientists, historians, professors, and explorers wrote, studied, and actively searched, to discover any trace of the ancient town, with little success.

Helike was founded sometime in the Bronze Age, becoming the principal city of Achaea. The poet Homer stated that the town of Helike "participated in the Trojan War with one ship." The visible clay statue shows the head of Poseidon, the city's patron, and the reverse of his trident.

The catastrophe was attributed to the anger of Poseidon, whose fury was magnified because the inhabitants of Helike had refused to give up some type of magical elixir to the Ionian colonists in Asia. According to some authorities, the inhabitants of Helike and Bura murdered the Ionian deputies.

After all the years of research that she had done in cuniform and other writings, Luci noticed that the writings on the pottery found in Santorini and the writing on the pictures of the shard that Nick had sent from Lima, Peru were precisely the same. She needed to find out how they all tied together.

***

@lucidefoix the only information you need is when and where I'm
going to kill your sister. Better decipher that shard fast, I'm losing
patience.

Luci whipped around, looking for anyone who might be texting
her. How could someone know where she was or what she was
doing?

February 10, 2020

"Sarah, Sarah, such a beautiful woman. You're not eating, honey.
My boss wouldn't like that," Ivan said.

"It doesn't matter," Sarah said, dully. "You're going to kill me
either way."

"No, I wouldn't kill you. My employer would be upset if you
died before you told me where the people of Helike sailed. She was
a close friend of your father at one time."

Ivan's home was located in an idyllic spot, providing a unique
glimpse of at least three different eco-systems. Crete is the largest
and most populous of the Greek islands, on the southern border of
the Aegean sea. People have lived on the island for over 130,000
years, and it was home to one of the most advanced civilizations
in the years BC. Their remains form a significant part of the
economy and cultural heritage of Greece, while the islanders have
retained their own local cultural traits. The Nikos at Heraklion and
Daskalogiannis airport at Chania serve international travelers. The
palace of Knossos, a Bronze Age settlement and ancient Minoan
city, can be found in Heraklion in Crete.

Sarah didn't answer. He wouldn't listen anyway. "Then she's
going to be horribly upset. I can't tell you what I don't know. We
haven't discovered it yet. That's why I was hired for the expedition. That's where Luci and I were heading when you kidnapped
me. Who is your employer?"

"It wouldn't be right for me to give you her name."

"I think her name is Bitch."

Ivan chuckled. "I won't tell her you're rude. She might take
offense. Then what would happen to you?" His smile faded. "No,
I don't like your condition at all." He brought the food closer.

"You have to eat to keep up your strength. Luci is helping to save you by translating that shard you gave to her. We have someone watching her right now. You're her incentive. When she gives us the information, we'll release you. I've also discovered you're not sleeping. I want no more tears and no more screaming." Ivan had been patient, and more forgiving than he had planned to be, but his patience was wearing out.

"Go to hell."

"I guess I'll be able to visit your father there, won't I?"

Sarah crumbled at the mention of her father. He was murdered by the mafia for not getting Solomon's seal to them. But how did this man know that?

"Now eat your food. I want you fresh and strong," he sighed and poured himself a glass of Macallan. The two hundred and fifty-year-old scotch was smooth and soothing and did much to bring him a sense of peace and calm. But even the delicate texture of the golden liquid would only take him away for so long.

She closed her eyes. She wanted to cry for herself and for Luci. What could possibly be happening? Sarah could shed no more tears, she was helpless. She had to keep up her strength. She had to get out of here and find Luci. She sat up and began to eat.

February 11, 2020

Max, an operative of the CIA, was stationed in Rome. He had seen the newspapers and had received a phone call from his long time friend, Nick de Foix.

"Max, Sarah has been kidnapped by Russians. They want an ancient clay pot with writings engraved on it. They have contacted Luci, demanding she decipher it quickly, or Sarah will die."

"What do you want me to do, Nick?"

"You're not retired yet, Max," he almost screamed. "Luci and I need your help in finding her before something horrible happens to her."

"No, I'm not retired." He paused for a moment, thinking about how this job had taken him away from the woman he loved, how much he had sacrificed. "Do you know where they've taken her?"

"I believe somewhere in Crete, but I don't know exactly where."

"I don't doubt that they need Sarah to leverage Luci."

"Can you use your contacts to find Sarah so we can get her out safely and stop Luci from giving them the location of the lost city?" As an afterthought, he said, "With the writings, of course."

"I can try to find Sarah, but it will take time, time that you don't have. Am I right?"

"But, you could find out more if we sent you to Crete, right?"

"Maybe." He gazed thoughtfully down at the whiskey he had poured himself. "Yes, probably." Luci hadn't returned his text. It might be an excellent opportunity to get hold of her and explain where he had been.

Nick wanted to strangle him. "You can find Sarah, right?"

"Yes, I think so."

"Let me make a few calls and see if my friend down in Crete knows of any Russian activity in the area."

"Is Luci in any danger?" Max said anxiously.

"Not as long as she is doing what the Russians want, but what I'm worried about is that the writing on the shard is from an ancient civilization, and I don't know if Luci can translate it in time."

"What is so important that the Russians want something bad enough to kidnap an American?"

"I believe the Russians kidnapped Sarah to get Luci to transcribe the writing on the pot, that might lead to clues to a lost city of a magical plant somewhere in South America."

"You don't believe in that hocus pocus stuff, do you? You know I'll be lucky to find Sarah alive."

"Please, Max, find her," Nick pleaded.

"I'll get on it right away," Max took a sip of his drink. I'll be lucky to get her out, at least in one piece, he thought.

February 1536

Calisto stood on the rocky ledge beside the waterfall inside the cave. She loved how the sun twinkled off the surface of the pool. A refreshing spray from the plunging water drifted over her body, cooling and drenching her skin.

Even though the cave smelled damp, and the acrid stench of mold clung to the back of her throat, Calisto loved her secret hideaway.

There were stairs down to the pool, which gave her a sense of overwhelming calm at the beauty that surrounded her.

Her cavern teemed with life. Insects scuttled from one hiding place to another. Underground passages that breathed out odors of damp earth with crevices to explore. In her *cueva*, with its strange setting, she considered herself part of the cave, part of the cavern.

From her perch high in the hollowed-out cave, she could see the sea mist clawing its way into the valley, and the temple the Helikes had begun to build. Around her, the day sparkled with life. Yet in just a few hours, the fog would wrap itself around everything in its path concealing the valley once again from the outside world.

She spent many hours lying by the pond or drawing pictures on the cave wall. Pictures that told stories about her family, about the animals and people that her Mitera cared for, and the golden mykite that could heal people. This was where their world began thousands of years ago. Here is where her ancestors breathed new life, and here was the magic elixir of life, and she would be an artist who told the story.

A distant sound startled her.

Her head snapped from side to side. She glanced around and listened. A strangled cry cut through her secret cave and sliced into her.

Calisto jumped off the rocky edge and plunged into the underground lake. She broke the surface of the crystal-clear pool. Gasping from the cold current, she swam a few strokes across the shimmering water and gazed out over a natural stone wall. Getting out, she ran through the rocky tunnel and clamored down the cliff into a shallow pond.

After wading across the stream and clawing over the golden-colored rocks, Calisto grabbed her linen tunic off a dangling branch and pulled it over her head. Holding up a hand to shield her eyes from the sun, she listened for the direction of the animal's cry. She leaped across the river and up the opposite riverbank. A young boy was struggling to break free. His rear foot was caught between two sunken boulders, blood caked his back right leg.

Calisto skidded to a halt and crept closer. The child was frightened and tried to escape. "Easy little one, it will be okay."

Whispering to keep him calm, she lay on top of the boulder, and her back rose in an uncomfortable arch. With both arms free, she tugged the rocks apart and freed the child.

Tucked under her arm, the boy trembled. His eyes rolled back in their sockets, a sign of death. With one final wrench, the skin lacerated along with her fingertips as she lifted the mangled foot from between the rocks.

Using her teeth, Calisto tore a strip off the bottom of her tunic. As she wrapped it around the wound, the boy's blood spurted over her hands and slithered down her arms.

Still whispering to keep the child calm, Calisto stood. The poor boy probably wouldn't survive. The wound was ugly, and the leg dangled in an awkward position. She had to go back to where she could protect the child's leg with water and the golden mykite that covered the rocks.

The Incan people prayed to their God, Patecatl, who condemned her and her mother for healing the sick who couldn't afford to see a doctor. So, they practised in secret. The herbal remedies from her secret cave had saved many of the local people from suffering. Now here was a boy, an Incan child, whom she could save.

Since her mother had continued the planting and cultivation of the mykite from their homeland off of the rocks beside the cave, her fame had grown. People traveled many days to consult her and stand outside the entrance waiting to be healed. She would treat the little boy. She sat beside him and carefully applied the golden mykite to the boy's wounds.

February 12, 2020

"We need to talk, Sarah," Ivan said.

She opened her eyes to see him kneeling beside her. "It doesn't do me any good to talk to you. You won't listen to me." Looking down, she noticed stitches in her arm.

"You hurt your arm when they dragged you into the van at the airport. It was looked at by a doctor. You're fine. Now I'll talk, you listen, and answer the questions."

"I don't know where the survivors of Helike went and I don't know anything about a lost city. I'm sure my sister is trying to decipher the clay shard and locate the city for you."

"That isn't the question." He gently stroked her cheek. "I've actually grown quite fond of you in these past few days. I don't believe I've felt this way with anyone before. What a brave, lovely woman you are."

She shuddered at his touch but didn't move. For the past few days, he'd been touching her, showing kindness. She had to stay strong or end up like Patty Hearst with Stockholm syndrome.

Ivan sighed. "Yes, it will bother me if I have to hurt you."

"Bull shit."

"It will Sarah," he said, almost reverently. "But you won't help me. Maybe a little persuasion will help."

"I can't help you. I've told you that. We found nothing on the expedition but a few clay pots."

Someone screamed nearby. It was ghastly, and she began to tremble.

Ignoring the sound, Ivan said, "I almost believe you. Yes, your sister has been deciphering the shard. So since you won't talk, and Luci isn't finding anything, you need to make a choice."

"What do you mean?"

"I'm sure you don't want your sister to be killed. I mean, you're the one with the computer skills. I believe with enough coaxing, we can convince Luci to speed up her efforts."

"Or what?"

"I can spare her and switch tactics with you. I'm going to regret this, I'm sure. I've grown quite fond of you."

She shook her head.

"You don't believe me? I'll prove it. We have just finished with a man who was obviously working for someone else in the American government. I can show you later if you like."

She leaned forward, her head shaking.

"I'll give you until tomorrow morning before we begin." He lowered his head and kissed her softly, kissed her cheek, smelling the sweet smell of her. "Do you know torture for women is rape? Sexual humiliation, I think. I can't do that to you..." Sarah looked up in hope at him only to have her hopes dashed. "So I've decided to turn you over to my cousin. Afterward, I believe he'll want to share you with his friends. You have until the morning to think about it."

Sarah watched him leave the house, panic rising inside her.

***

Luci left the library with Sarah's shard, no further in deciphering it. She'd had an epiphany and raced down to the archeological site connected to Sarah's work.

Most of the coastline on Crete consisted of undulating sand, which was vulnerable to erosion, and unusually harsh weather. As Luci walked down to the site, she noticed a cist recently exposed by a storm. She pulled out her trowel and began removing silty sand. She realized she should call the Greek government as this was a significant find, but her sister's life was on the line. She had no idea what was going on. Still, the last text warned that within twenty-four hours, Sarah was going to be given to a man who enjoyed torturing and raping women.

Luci had been working in this area for the last couple of days. It was a grueling task to undertake alone. She couldn't call on Sarah, and Max was out of the picture. She had texted him, but he never replied. Luci really did need his help. If she had to be honest about everything, though, she never did tell him about carrying his baby.

Out of the corner of her eye, she spied a man walking toward her. "What are you doing?" he asked.

He looked familiar, but she had difficulty bringing up where she had seen him before. "I'm visiting the island. My family went out to eat, so I thought I'd come down here and build a sand castle," Luci answered, covering up the cist. "Is it against the law, sir?"

"No, not building a sandcastle, but this is a dig site, as you well know, Luci."

Her face drained of any color at the mention of her name.

"My men will be back, and we want to make sure you know that tomorrow Sarah is in a lot of trouble, and I'm sure you understand that if you don't give us something by then, we won't need her anymore. Do you understand?"

Luci noticed that beside his right foot an object in the sand had surfaced with his weight. "Yes, sir. Please don't hurt her."

"That's entirely up to you. See that you translate that shard you have in your possession." He walked away.

She moved over to where he had been standing and used her trowel to uncover the object. It couldn't be...after all this time. She couldn't be this lucky...

It was a piece of pottery and, using her hands, she began pushing the sand away as the tide came in. She couldn't wait any longer, she had to pull out the object or risk losing it to the ocean. Slipping it into her pocket, she walked away.

***

"Your time is up, Sarah. What's your answer?" Ivan pulled her to her feet.

"We found nothing on the last expedition. I've said this a million times, you just won't listen."

"Probably because I don't believe you. My friend is anxiously awaiting your arrival." He licked the side of her face.

Sarah grimaced.

"You're so pretty. I've truly grown quite fond of you. Are you sure you won't tell me the location of a lost city?" He pulled her closer to him. "I'll give you a hint, gold, Pizarro."

She shook her head.

"Oh, Sarah, Sarah, Sarah, what am I going to do with you?" He lowered his head and softly placed his mouth on hers.

She bit down hard on his lower lip.

"Whore!" His fist flew out. It struck her in the face and knocked her to the floor. His lip was torn and bleeding. He jerked her back up off the floor. "You have an appointment to keep. I'm sure you'll be a lot more friendly after he gets through with you."

**

Oh, my God! That's him! Luci realized the identity of the man who had just left. It was the blue-eyed man with light brown hair who was on the flight from France not four months before. Her nerves went into overdrive. He was also the guy who had kidnapped Sarah.

She moved around, trying to go undetected as she packed up her belongings and shoved the shiny object into her backpack. He stopped, turned around, and gazed right into her eyes. She knew he had seen her put something into her bag, and by his look, knew that she recognized him.

"Yes, the woman who I traveled with from France. You've found something, haven't you? Hand it over to me right now," he said, walking back.

"I'm looking for clues to help my sister. It's the piece of shard Sarah gave me containing an unknown language from an expedition she was on. But you know that already, don't you? By the way, what's your name?"

"It doesn't matter what my name is, and yes, for a time, Sarah and I were colleagues, but I had to quit the expedition. I've gone to historians and philologists, but none have been able to figure out what the writing on the shard means." Xander drew a piece of pottery from a pocket and handed it to her. "And now the Russians have your sister."

"Where did you find this?" Luci curiously flipped the piece of pottery one way and another, trying to get a better look at the writing. She was interested, but her fear was greater. They had Sarah. "I'm going back to my room, I'll work on deciphering this with the other pieces. I'll call."

"The same place that Sarah found her shard. Thank you, Luci. We really appreciate your help with this. Can I have the pottery back along with whatever you put in your bag?" he asked, smiling. "On second thought, let me formally introduce myself, my name is Xander Deux. I don't want you to forget me."

Luci slapped the piece of pottery back into his hand, but it was with great effort. "Wait. Can I take some pictures of it first? I can think about it on the flight."

"Certainly. It will keep you reminded of us and what we hope to find. The clock is ticking, though; Sarah's life hangs in the balance."

"You keep saying we, who is we? Are you here to help her?"

"That's up to her. The Russians pay much better than a scientific expedition."

Luci took her iPhone from her purse and snapped pictures. Concentrating on the images, she became startled when her phone beeped another reminder about her call.

@lucidefoix I'm watching

***

Flustered, Luci looked away for a moment and didn't hear what Xander was saying. "I'm sorry, could you repeat that?"

"I believe we can be of help to one another."

"In what way?" She had a horrible feeling that this was not going to work in favor of locating Sarah.

"I'm looking for a lost city in Peru, in the Amazon jungle near Cuzco, many people before me have tried and failed to locate it."

"So you're a benevolent kind of guy? I thought your interest was helping your friends, the Russians. What are you really looking for?"

"Actually, I'm looking for the Seven Caves of Gold in Peru. The Russians want them, but you're going to help me first, Luci."

"Now, why would I do that? Will you get Sarah away from the Russian?" Luci said evenly.

Xander grabbed at Luci. "You're going to get to know me quite well."

***

Xander's thoughts ran wild in remembrance of that day not so long ago. He enjoyed watching Luci struggle in the pool, to catch her breath, to grab onto the rocks. That was an added bonus to stick one to Max. The best thing, she didn't know who he was or what he had done to her.

Xander reached out and grabbed Luci's hair and tried to throw her to the ground.

***

Luci did a roundhouse kick to Xander's head. He quickly loosened his grip on her hair.

Knowing he was losing the fight, he said, "From what I understand, my friends found shards of pottery on Sarah and believe the writing on them will give a location to where the remaining people of Helike finally ended up. They think it's somewhere in Peru. We must find the site. It could help locate the remaining members of a lost civilization. Soon we might not need either of you."

"You mean the Seven Caves of Gold—that's what you're interested in, aren't you? Your friends, are they really in it to discover a lost civilization, or find the gold?" Luci questioned.

Ignoring her, he said, "Your sister is in a lot of trouble. I'm here to help persuade you to help them."

"But I haven't deciphered anything. I'm trying." She said nothing about the information that she recently discovered. "I want Sarah back. She has the computer skills that could help me decipher some of these shards. You know I would do anything to save her." She hesitated a moment, then added, "But how do I know you and your so-called friends haven't already killed her?"

"Good question. Have you received any pieces of her yet?"

"No!"

"Well, my lovely Luci, you have your answer."

"Why Peru, why not Italy? Couldn't the survivors have landed there?" she questioned, slowly getting off the ground and picking up her backpack.

"I think many people did find their way to Italy. But we also feel there were a few who went further, we believe to Peru."

Luci persisted, "Couldn't the pottery be located somewhere else?"

He nodded. "No, we found a map etched on the shard I just showed you. But you know that, please don't take me for a fool. The sooner you translate all the pottery we have given you we will have our answer, or most of it anyway. One of our philologists translated the shard from a woman stating that she and her husband, Shira, took a clay pot from a cave on a cliff before the earthquake."

"I have twenty-four hours left to save Sarah," she said, buying time. "I haven't found anything here. Maybe a piece of the shard was already found, maybe taken somewhere else by other people.

In my research, I heard about the disappearance of a man named Flammel and a golden pot that he had in France."

"Already checked it out, and it is meaningless. I need you to come with me so you can translate the shard for me." Xander stealthily moved closer to her.

"What about Sarah?"

"The sooner you help me, the sooner Sarah will be free."

Luci's backpack was heavy. If she left with him, both she and Sarah would be lost. She needed to get away from this man.

A massive wave crashed onto the shore. It startled Xander, and he turned to watch. Luci heaved her bag at his head. He went down hard. She took off running without her bag, never looking back.

Luci ran all the way back to her rental car, left everything but her handbag at the hotel, and set off for the airport to South America.

February 13, 2020

"It's time, Sarah. According to my friend who visited Luci just recently, she hasn't found anything." Ivan pulled her to her feet. "My number one is anxiously awaiting. We don't want to make her wait too long for the information. She'll be furious. Are you ready for your big date?"

Sarah didn't answer. She felt like she was going to throw up, and her legs felt wobbly. They walked out of the house, the sun was bright. She blinked hard, unable to see after being in the darkened room for so long. She stumbled to the ground, Ivan grabbed her and pushed her toward a storage facility a short distance away.

He pulled open the door that was sheltered from the ocean by huge rocks. "Here she is, Sergei." He pushed her into the small room. "Don't kill her. Everything else is allowed." He touched his lip, "even advised."

"It can't be. What are you doing here, Sergei?" Sarah recognized him and knew he was dangerous.

"I've been waiting for you for so long, Sarah. I saw the looks you gave me on the expedition." Sergei smiled, getting to his feet.

"You're crazy. You were a deckhand. What are the Russians paying you?"

"Actually, quite a lot. And now you are the icing, or should I say cherry, on top?"

Ignore him. Fight him. Try to get away. This was her only hope. Once Ivan came back, there would be little left of her.

"Tell me you want me," he said. "Tell me you want to suck my dick. Tell me you want me to fuck you." When she said nothing, his grip tightened on her. "Beg me, whore."

Sarah swung her knee up and connected with his balls. As he groaned, she ran toward the entrance, knocking down a table, breaking a gas latern. He caught her before she reached the door and slapped her. She fell to the floor. He kicked her in the head.

Her body ached, and her head rang as he flipped her over. She could barely see him through the haze of pain.

"You run from me?" He took his knife out of his waistband. "I'll make sure you don't make that mistake again." He plunged the blade into her right calf.

Sarah screamed, pain ripping through her.

"That's right." He pulled out the knife and stabbed it into the earth next to them, burying the point in the dirt. "Ivan will love hearing you scream. I'll keep this knife next to me in case I feel like cutting your breasts just a little." Sergei tore open her blouse and cut off her bra. Maybe you'd like me to start with your breasts..." He bent his head and touched a nipple with his tongue. His face flushed. "You bit Ivan until he bled. Do you think he'd be pleased if I bit this pretty nipple and made you bleed?"

Glass shards were within reach.

Pain tore at her nipple as his teeth sank savagely into it. The moan she gave was no pretense.

He lifted his head and licked the blood off her breast. "Now the other one." His teeth bit deep.

She cried out. She arched her buttocks upward while stretching for a shard of glass. Grabbing one, she plunged it into his side.

He screamed like a mad dog; his head jerked up.

Sarah pushed away and scrambled to her knees.

The shard hadn't stopped him. He grabbed her ankles and reached for his gun. "Bitch."

He scrambled toward her, but a man appeared and kicked him in the side. He grabbed Sergei's knife, pulled out his gun and shot Sergei in the arm. Her rescuer clipped him with the gun along side his head for good measure. "That will give us time to get you out of here."

Sarah stared, unable to move. Everything happened so fast. She hadn't recognized the man until that very moment. His crystal blue eyes held such intensity.

Max.

"Grab the gun and any ammunition you can find." Max dragged the huge body toward the bed and dropped a blanket over him. "I'll be back."

"Wait. Max, please don't leave me here."

"The CIA sent me to get you, Sarah. Put your clothes on and grab the gun. I'll be right back. Then we're out of here."

Sarah hurriedly stood up and dressed. She fell over in agony, pain shot up her leg. She had forgotten about the knife wound. It was now throbbing. She rolled up her pant leg. It was ugly, but the blood had stopped. She limped across the room and grabbed the AK-47.

Max returned. "We can go now." He carried a rifle and a backpack, one that Luci had given him. He reached into the pack and pulled out a hat. "Wear it."

***

Later

"You okay?" Max yelled back at her.

"Yes." But that was a lie. She was exhausted and shaking from all the walking they had done. "How much farther?"

"Just up ahead…I hid a motorcycle," Max said. "Keep moving."

Keep moving, easy to say, she thought numbly. She'd been lucky just to stay on her feet.

"Do you need help?" Max asked.

Yes, but if Max helped her, it would slow them both down, and they needed to get away as quickly as possible.

"No, I'm fine, but thanks. I've got to keep moving."

"Don't fall. We're almost there."

Hot, so hot.

"Come on, Sarah."

Max was back beside her. He slipped his arm around her waist. "We're almost there. Just a couple more feet."

In the distance, she could just make out the outline of a Harley. "Thank God."

Max helped Sarah onto the back of the bike. He gave her a bottle of water and turned on the engine. "I've got an airplane waiting. It will take you to South America. Luci and your uncle Nick will be waiting."

"They know?"

***

"Sarah's gone, Ivan. I was on top of her ready to fuck her brains out, but someone broke into the storage facility."

"Shit, you were in that room for a long time. Was she too much for you to handle?" Ivan heard something in the distance, the engine of a motorcycle. He should have expected it. "Dammit, go tend to your wound. How long do you think they've been gone?"

"Maybe ten minutes at most."

"Alexy," he ordered the man standing outside his factory office. "Get the men. We're going after our precious cargo."

"Think about it for a minute. You've had her for several weeks, and she didn't break. Maybe she doesn't have any information."

"Your point being?"

"Forget about her. Find Luci. She'll lead us to the Golden Caves."

He lifted his hand where Sarah had bit him and wanted payback. "That bitch will be found. Now get the men and go after her. I haven't finished with her yet. Sergei, did you get a good look at the men who attacked you?"

"There was only one man, I'm sure of that, but he was a professional. He came from behind me; he was good. He could have killed me but stopped short."

***

Sarah had drifted off to sleep, it was a restless sleep, but at this point, that's all he could hope for. He knelt and tucked the blanket closer around her, then rose and headed for the cockpit of Nick's jet. They would be landing soon.

February 1536

Calisto took the little boy toward her home but was waylaid by her uncle. He stood on the outskirts of the village, waving to her to come walk with him back to his home.

"Calisto, you must come and have a cup of coffee that I've just prepared." He entered his home; she and the child followed. "And what do we have here?"

"I found this little boy in the cavern. His leg was stuck between rocks. Look at the deep cut he has."

"He will be useless to his people, Calisto. It would have been better to let him die, the Incans will have no use for him, and they will sacrifice him."

"Mitera will cure him. She can cure anyone."

"Shh," he said, looking frightened. "Don't let the people of the village hear you."

"But, Uncle…"

"No, listen Calisto, I have bad news."

February 20, 2020

As she sat upright in the airplane seat, Luci's heart pounded against her ribs. Her body seemed to be suddenly filled with wriggling eels. All of this reminded her of the death of her parents and grandparents, and the lengths people would go to for money.

Shards of pottery, and best of all, was the picture sent by her uncle Nick that told her the approximate location of where the Helikes landed in Peru. This was intriguing, and yet she'd been in this same place before. But that was with Max. He was always there; she felt protected by him, and now she was alone.

Could this secret city contain a miracle cure for all people and change the world, open it up for more opportunities and remedies, or was it just gold or just a myth?

The plane hit an air pocket. The co-pilot moving down the aisle lurched against her seat. "Excuse me," he said.

Luci briefly looked up and realized she had to use the restroom as well.

She got up from her seat and shoved the bathroom door shut with her tennis shoe. Using her longest nail, Luci plonked the lid down and wriggled onto the toilet seat. She rummaged in her handbag and fished out an aspirin thinking about the cryptic note on the plane, and how she had sensed that someone familiar had left it for her. Their paths had collided for a reason.

On the seat, she swung around, faced the sink, and filled her chest with a deep gulp of air. She went into a coughing fit.

Luci received a text from Sarah. With Max's help, Sarah had escaped and was heading to Lima to meet up with her.

Luci had texted Sarah about the *text troll* and how the threats were escalating. *I don't want any crazies pulling anything on us.* Luci didn't want to say anything about what Sarah had just gone through. Let her bring it up in her own time.

"I know what you're thinking, Luci, and don't worry. We'll have guards plugged in."

"Nick said he had the perfect man for the job."

"That's a huge relief."

***

"Alexander Treblinka recently left the Russian army to start his own business. He put together a smaller outfit than the big companies, but they were all ex-mercenaries. He may not have all the latest gadgets, but you can trust him to keep us safe," Luci informed her.

"Thank Nick for me. I appreciate his help." Sarah didn't want to talk about what she had gone through; it was too raw in her mind.

"It's the least he can do. Especially now that we find the Russians are after a Lost City of Gold. What they don't know is that I've deciphered the writing on the shard, and Uncle will be meeting us at the Marriott Hotel. I'll have it, and the approximate location of that city, by the time he arrives."

***

@lucidefoix you don't know where we are right now, but be afraid.

February 1536

Time slowed as Calisto waited for her uncle to explain the bad news. Her pulse quickened.

"There is a problem for healers, sweet one."

"Is that because Ahuitzoti, the new leader of the Incans, is against women healers?"

"*Nai*, yes."

"But we're only helping heal the poor. We're doing no harm."

"I'm sorry, little one, but the Incans do not feel this way. They say you are a Tlahuelpuchi—a vampire witch. Women in the nearby village are being murdered. You and Athena must leave quickly before the warriors come and take you away."

"This is my home, my ancestors. Pateras helped to build this city and wanted me to safeguard the secrets of the cavern. Besides, where would Mitera and I go? Everything I know and love is here."

"If you stay, all of us here are in danger, Calisto."

In the distance, Calisto could hear someone screaming. She raced out the door. "Please let me leave the child here. I will come back to him, but I have to hurry."

February 21, 2020

Sarah had fallen asleep. Max pulled a blanket from the overhead compartment and put it around her, watching as she twitched uneasily. Reminders of what she had gone through.

The flight from Crete to Rome hadn't taken long. Through the years, Max had grown accustomed to the luxury of flying on private jets; it was something that never got old. Every time he had to fly on a commercial flight, he longed for the decadence of comfort.

"How is she?" Dan, the pilot, inquired.

"I'm afraid she's just barely hanging in there."

"What happened to her?"

"I don't know, and she won't talk about it."

"Are we taking her to headquarters?"

"I think that might be a bad idea. They'd push her over the edge," Max responded. He'd been through this sort of scenario before.

"They need the information on the Russians. You can't get involved. Besides, they want to know about the writing on the pottery."

"I know, but I think she needs some downtime after what she's been through."

"So, what are you going to do?"

"Take her to Rome with us and then to where her family is staying in South America."

"That's not our orders."

"But it's Luci's uncle's jet."

The pilot nodded solemnly and went back to his cockpit.

Once they landed, Dan took off to get the car. Sarah watched him leave. She listened as Max's boots kicked up the dust and gravel as he walked towards her. "Were you trying to get rid of him?"

He nodded. "I have to talk to you before he gets back."

"Why?"

"That car on the runway is intended to take you to Rome. Once you get there, you're going to be grilled. The US Ambassador wants to know about the shard Nick somehow got his hands on. And they're going to ask what happened in Crete."

Every muscle in her body tensed. "No. I'm not reliving that."

"Then you need to get back on the jet and take off for South America. You need to see a doctor and rest. Here comes the car. What do you want to do?" Max asked.

Sarah hobbled back to the jet, climbed the stairs, and told the pilot to take off for South America. She was going back to the real world. Ugly memories and nightmares would always invade her mind and might not ever stop if she stayed with Max here in Rome.

But not now, not this minute. Sarah lay back against the cushioned seats and gazed out at the moonlight filtering through the window. She felt at peace, knowing she would be back with her family. She wouldn't be alone anymore.

***

Luci flinched at the sight of a text message from the unknown texter. What the hell? She read the message:

@lucidefoix The news. Watch now! ABC Exclusive! Poor Max!

The image of bodies with bloody slashes around their necks flew into her mind. Luci sprinted back inside her hotel room, grabbed the TV remote with clammy hands, and flicked the TV to the first news program she found. A red Breaking News ticker-tape ran across the bottom of the screen:

Rome, Italy. Vatican City has been bombed.

Many casualties, an embassy attaché has died.

Luci screamed, eyes glued to the scenes playing out in front of her. Police cars lined the Vatican center. Their blue lights flashed a warning to locals and tourists to stay away. Ten ambulances almost jackknifed beside each other, and their back doors ajar, with paramedics rushing up and down the steep slope. Two of them carried a stretcher. A white sheet concealed a body.

Luci let out a groan and covered her mouth with her hands.

Time seemed to tick in thick mud.

Max can't be dead, not now. Not ever. Relax. Maybe he wasn't there. There was so much left unsaid between them. She wondered if she and Max could have overcome the distance between them. She had wanted to say so much to him, and not leave it as she had.

As she watched the news, Luci's teeth sawed against her thumbnail in time to the beat of her pounding heart.

Debris was scattered across the piazza, including what looked like a bumper from a van split in two. A small suitcase with clothes flapping in the breeze lay next to the entrance. A child's doll left in the street.

Far below, a truck had slammed against an electric pylon. Its nose had crumpled into the windscreen as though the vehicle had been an accordion crushed against a wall. Watching in horror as the scenes of devastation marred the majesty of the cathedral, Luci heard the journalist repeat the story.

"Breaking news. The Vatican has been targeted by a left-wing extremist who has taken credit for this massacre of innocents in this holiest of holy cities. We have just learned that there have been fifty-two killed and over a hundred injured in this melee. This is a sad day for the world."

Once again, the camera panned over the wreckage of the cathedral, and people being helped to the ambulances by other injured people. The journalist was silent for a long moment as the image repeated the scene of the medical team carrying a small sheet-covered body to one of the ambulances. "A five-year-old girl, visiting the cathedral with her family..."

The news anchors asked the polizia, "What do we know of the vehicle?"

"The Mercedes truck was laden with explosives. The investigators will do a thorough examination of the wreck."

"Do we know what happened?"

"Not officially. It's rumored by some of the tourists that the truck drove through the gates. Because of the logo on the side of the truck, many believed he was delivering something. But I've been told by the Italian *polizia* we'll hear more when they're ready to inform us."

"Thank you, Brian. A sad day indeed."

As the anchor moved on to the next story, Luci sat motionless, chills coursing through her as if someone was strumming her nerves like a guitar. Guilt competed with the horror of the images, and together they caused havoc in her mind.

Pinning her arms around her stomach to stop nausea from creeping up. Luci stood to pull herself together. Her hands trembled with regret.

Why hadn't she texted Max back? Why did he want to meet her in Crete? Did he know something was about to happen?

But how could he have known about his own death?

**

Hearing a knock on her hotel room door, Luci gaped at the man filling her doorway. At least six feet six, big and ugly, he held out his hand. "Miss de Foix. I'm Alexander Treblinka. Please call me, Alexy."

He looked more like a gang banger than a personal security guard, but she offered him a seat. Distinctly uncomfortable in his jacket, he took it off and slung it over the arm of the sofa. "First, I need to understand the nature of the threat. How did this start and how long has it been going on?"

"I can show you my phone."

"I'll need to assess how much of your information is publicly available, and I'd like full details of which social media this person is targeting."

"There's no time. Sarah and I need protection now."

"Miss de Foix."

"Please, call me Luci."

"Okay, Luci, it's my job to put you and your sister's safety first. I'll put you under surveillance, but the other information will help me create a profile of the stalker and build evidence against him to give to the police."

She nodded. "Yes, of course."

"I recommend you delay any trips you are planning and stay right here with your uncle."

"No way. I'm leaving right now. I'm picking up Sarah at Lima airport. Next week we're all going on an archeological expedition into Cuzco."

"I strongly suggest you rethink this."

"You can go with Sarah and me to protect us both if you want, but I am going."

He stretched and rose to his feet. "I'd better get on with some security measures. Can I have your keys?"

"Why?"

"So, I can set up alarms in yours and Sarah's hotel rooms right now."

"Oh, okay." She strode to the desk, fiddled in her purse, and finally found the keys to give to him.

"Is anyone following us while we're here...you know...in case someone tries something?"

"Someone will be here within minutes while I go shopping, Miss, umm, Luci."

"Thank you. That's a relief."

"Don't worry. You're safe now."

"From your lips to God's ears."

***

@lucidefoix watch out bitch...

March 1536

As the full moon lit her path through the woods, Calisto ran through the night. In her mind, she created stories of a young girl being a goddess to wild animals. She was a princess in her own kingdom, healing and nurturing her people.

Her Mitera insisted on gathering the mykite at night to prevent strangers from seeing her carrying bunches of smelly herbs. She wasn't afraid of the dark; she was more fearful of what would happen if the Aztec warrior in the village just outside the cave ever found her.

Calisto lived with the fear her uncle had told her: the healer being murdered. Every day she rose early to pray her secret would never be found.

Ambling along the meadow towards the cave, Calisto gazed at their moonlit home with pride. Outbuildings sprawled around the cottage. Long shadows from the animals' shed reached out and molded their distorted fingers onto the farm's most revered outbuilding: her papa's workshop.

After Patera had been trapped in a neighbor's home that collapsed, her mother refused to clear out his tools. She often sat amongst his things and talked to his spirit. Calisto wished she had known about the healing power of the mykites at that time. Her mother said that when she spoke to Patera, a dove always appeared. Eleni told her these birds only had one mate. Sometimes her mother said strange things.

A candle burned brightly inside their home, welcoming her to the thatched cottage with smoke coming out of the chimney. The thatch suddenly seemed to lean to one side and frown at her.

The front door stood ajar.

Calisto's pulse quickened. Mitera always insisted on the door being shut to keep the heat inside. Then raucous laughter spilled from the cottage. Calisto stopped.

Men.

Only evil men laughed that way. Loud and vulgar. The harsh tones disturbed the peace.

These were not the sounds of people from her village.

Panic gripped her.

Where was her Mitera?

February 22, 2020

Luci had been so engrossed in typing on her laptop, she hadn't noticed the day had long ago slipped into night.

The sounds of the city were calming, familiar. Car horns tooted and taxi cabs blasted in return as Lima took on a new persona. Without looking, Luci knew the vibrant nightlife would be aglow with light spilling out of the many bars, restaurants, and ground floor offices lining the Ovalo Higuereta.

Someone entered her room. Turning around, she dropped the laptop and ran to Sarah, who was on crutches. She threw her arms around her. "I've been so worried about you. What happened? Where've you been?"

"Oh, Luci, I'm so sorry. There has been so much that has happened." She broke down.

"You're okay, right?"

"I just need to rest for a while."

Luci looked down at Sarah's bandaged leg. "What happened, Sarah?"

Sarah looked different, the bones of her face were bold and well-defined. Her lips were full but beautifully formed. Her deep-dark set eyes shone with a spirit Luci hadn't seen before.

"It's only a scratch on my leg. I need some time to process everything that happened to me. Before I go to my room, I want to tell you that Max and I were in Rome. He left the jet with this other man and headed for the Vatican. I saw on the news that a bombing had occurred. I'm worried about Max. He saved my life. If it weren't for him, I don't know what would have happened to me, Luci. Have you heard anything from him?" she choked out.

"No, I'm worried as well. I hope and pray he's okay. I keep texting him to no avail. Let's see if Uncle Nick knows anything." She put an arm around her sister.

Nick was watching the news on the television. Luci and Sarah sat down next to him, hoping for a phone call from Max. After an hour and no call, Luci decided to go back to her room, concerned that her stalker and Sarah's kidnapper were out there, watching, and waiting for an opportunity...to do what, she didn't have a clue.

Walking down the hallway, she opened the door just a crack. Sarah bolted upright and screamed. Luci flew into the room, her heart pounding as if trying to break free. "It's all right, Sarah, you're here now with Nick and me."

"How long have you been there?" Sarah asked.

"I was walking to my room and checked on you. Would you like a glass of water?"

Sarah realized her throat was dry. "It's okay, I can get it."

"I'll stay here until you're ready to rest. Drink your water. I'll wait until you tell me what happened to you in Greece. Then I'll leave and let you go back to sleep. Though I don't promise I won't look in on you."

***

Later that evening, animated chatter and loud laughter drifted through the door. The tinkling sounds of glasses could be heard by Nick and their expedition crew. Luci was well aware that her family wanted her to find the Seven Golden Caves. But did she? Luci had lost so many friends and family. The thought of more being killed tore at her heart. She longed for what she once had and lost, Max and their baby.

Luci picked up her laptop and closed it. She walked down the stairs to the hotel restaurant for a bite to eat. As she descended, she thought for the hundredth time about the latest tweet: *Watch your back, bitch, I'm watching, and the bodyguard can't protect you from me.* Luci saw her guard following her but wasn't sure if she felt safe or not.

I pray Max is alive, and maybe we can start over, Luci thought.

***

Luci marched into the living room of her Uncle Nick's hotel suite and spotted him speaking with Sarah.

She listened to Sarah tell Nick what she had gone through. Her heels tapped across the floor.

"Max shot at him."

Luci rubbed a sudden hive of gooseflesh.

Sarah smiled at Luci. "He saved my life, Luci."

Eyeing Sarah suspiciously, she asked, "Do you know where he's been?"

"That was the first I saw or heard of him since France."

"No phone calls, only one text from him."

"You know he works for the CIA. There were things he couldn't get out of, like now, saving Sarah. And that was dangerous and important to all of us, Luci," Uncle Nick said, trying to bring the tension down a notch.

As Sarah left, muttering that she was going to set up her computer, Luci's phone beeped. Her breakfast turned in her stomach. Luci's finger twitched as it hovered over the message.

Oh, God. What now?

@lucidefoix your loverboy will be dead soon enough.

Take deep breaths, Luci told herself.

Sarah was in a cold sweat. Running a damp cloth over her face, she poured a glass of water and took a sip with hands tightened on the water glass to keep them from shaking.

She had to be tougher, she couldn't allow Ivan to break her. Thankfully there hadn't been a nightmare for three days now.

Sarah's strength was returning, she would go on the expedition. Rule number one: keep a hold of herself and stop thinking...

A knock came at the door.

***

Luci exited the silver SUV at the entrance to a gray, palatial hotel, phone glued to her ear. At the same time, she lugged shopping bags and listened to messages. Luci ran headfirst into a wheelchair.

"Whoa!" The occupant raised his hands and leaned back.

That's when she recognized him! "Max, Max, wait, what...Oh my God, you're alive."

"Calm down, Luci, it's okay."

Even though his lopsided boyish grin sent waves of excitement to her nerve endings, she couldn't let on what effect he still had on her. Without meaning to she snapped at him, "Why didn't you call me? I thought you were dead."

"Luci, I had work to do, and I was hurt in the explosion."

Running her fingers through her hair, she reached out to Max, but he flinched away. Puzzled, she asked, "What's wrong, Max?"

"I wanted a better place to talk to you. I'm okay. My leg was just hit by some glass. I'm fine."

"So, you made the decision to exclude me from your life! I would always be there for you, I love you, and you know it."

"Maybe then, but now…What do you mean I wasn't there for you?"

"What do *you* mean?" Luci answered cautiously.

"Sarah told me everything. I should have been there with you."

"You're really stupid."

"You're young. You can have a life with someone."

"But I have chosen to have a life, a life with you—not anyone else."

Max began a coughing fit; he was turning blue. Luci ran to him and put her hand on his shoulders. "Let go, Luci, I need some water," he said, dejectedly as he got himself under control.

"Max, please listen to me."

"I came here to tell you to forget me, get on with your life." He turned around and got into a car.

"You're giving up on us? Is that it?" Luci screamed.

"Let it go, Luci, just let it go."

Without another word, she straightened, grabbed her bags, and rushed back toward the hotel. As she reached the entrance, her phone beeped to announce another text had arrived.

***

When U R finished with lover boy @ the hotel, I'll be waiting.

February 23, 2020

"You're crazy, Luci. Why do you love him so much?" Luci said to herself, driving over to meet Nick and Sarah at the Marriott El Convento. It was a chic hotel with rooms in a two-hundred-year-old restored convent built around Inca ruins.

Luci needed to get her luggage from the trunk of the rental car. She had forgotten them with all the talk with Max.

Luci's glare lifted from the stalker's text and moved into the lobby.

She jabbed the last number dialed and panted into it, "Are you there, Alexy?"

"Everything okay, Luci?"

She exhaled and said, "I just got another message."

"You need to contact Twitter. They have rules about this kind of thing happening."

Before she could answer, another message came through:

@lucidefoix I'm not going away. I can always retake Sarah.

Luci gasped. It's as if this person knew her every move.

"I'm in my room," Alexy said. "Do you want me to come up to your room?"

"No, I'll be fine, I'll see you later." Luci's shoulders shook with the thought of losing Max again. Tears streaked down her face. *You may be okay with this, Max, but I'm not. I won't give up on us, ever.*

***

Xander tossed a fifty-dollar bill at the driver and stepped out of the black cab into the early morning drizzle. A wave of foul-smelling heat pumping out the smell of petrol fumes rose from under the vehicle.

He hated traveling in cabs. They stank, and who knew what slob had sat on the seat minutes before? But it was the only way to move around in this city.

He had finally arrived in Lima and had booked a room not far from where Luci and Sarah were staying. One of his men would be on the expedition they were taking, and he would be close by, waiting and watching.

March 2, 2020

"Everything we've been able to piece together from the shards so far seems to point to the jungles in Cuzco," Nick said.

Everyone was in agreement across the table. Sarah seemed a bit apprehensive after what she had been through.

Luci grabbed her go bag off the counter and took it to the dining room table where they were just finishing cheese blintzes and coffee. Everyone gazed at her curiously as she pulled out the shard from Crete. Setting the piece on the table, she told them of her find and how she escaped Xander.

"Oh my God. Did you find it, the one with the location—when were you going to tell us?" Sarah asked excitedly. "Xander works with the Russians? Figures..."

"Yes, he does. This shard is only for our eyes."

"It looks like it's glowing!" Nick said.

"If it only glows, what good is it except maybe as a nightlight?" Sarah exclaimed.

"Funny, but in the taxi, I noticed that it has fungi—almost golden in color—attached to it."

"Do you believe that the writing is telling us where the Seven Golden Caves is located?" Nick asked.

"I'm not sure. It doesn't have coordinates; it has dots and lines, but we'll know more after we set off into the jungle. That will be the test."

"When do we leave?" Sarah asked apprehensively.

"First of next week, but you're not going," Nick said.

"But..."

"You need to be our eyes and ears right here in this room. You're the one who can use the GPS and keep tabs on our team."

"I understand. I don't have a problem with that. I just wish I could use the drone to help navigate you away from any difficulties."

"So do I. Are you sure there isn't a way to have Sarah come with us?" asked Luci.

"Nick, my leg is fine. I can keep my eyes and ears open with my laptop and GPS tracker. Like I said, I can't use the drone, and I really think I'd better help working with you all than staying here."

"I'm not comfortable with this, Sarah. I'm concerned about those men who captured you."

"Being here at the hotel by myself is not safer, Nick. I don't think I'm the only target. They want Luci as well. I was bait. Thank God, Max rescued me. How's he doing, by the way?"

"I think he'd like to be out there with us. Now let's go out for a nice dinner," Luci said, avoiding the topic of Max.

"I'll call him and see if he would like to help us," Nick said.
Luci walked out of the room, slamming the door behind her.

@lucidefoix it won't be long now.

***

Getting into their taxi, Sarah explained the history of the Incan civilization that arose from the highlands of Peru in the 15th century. It kept her mind from drifting to the terrifying days she spent in Crete. "Starting in 1438, they began conquering lands surround-ing the heartland of Cuzco, creating the largest empire in pre-Columbian America. But the landing of the Spanish conquistadors marked an end of the short-lived Inca Empire."

"Okay, enough of the history lesson, this is our last night in the city, and I'm starved," Nick said.

"Tell the taxi driver to stop here. This restaurant looks interest-ing. Mmm, Cicciolina," Luci said.

Nick, Luci, and Sarah entered the restaurant and headed for the bar to wait for their table.

After ordering a margarita and some tapas, Luci asked, "Sarah, since you've been studying the Incas, what happened between Pizarro and Atahualpa where the Seven Golden Caves is supposed to be?"

"It really goes much further back than that. Let's start with the name of the city we're headed for, Cuzco. The name of this city is Quesqu, its origin is found in Cicciolina, the Aymara language. It means 'Rock of the owl' relating to the city's myth of the Ayar Siblings. According to legend, Ayar Awqu acquired wings and flew to the site of the future city; there, he was changed into a rock to mark the possession of the land by his Ayllu (lineage). Nick, you know more about the myth. Tell Luci."

"The Ayar Oce stood up, displayed a pair of giant wings, and said he should stay at Guanacaure as an idol to speak with their father the Sun. Ayar Oche rose in flight toward the heavens. He returned and told Ayar that from then on, he was to be named Manco Capac. Manco Capac, with four women, planted some of their lands with a healing herb. It is said that they took the herb from the cavern, which Manco Capac named Mykite, which means those of origin because...they came out of that cave."

"Wow, how long have you guys been researching the Incas?" asked Luci.

"We did it to arm ourselves against what happened to other people like us who were exploring."

"What do you mean, Nick?"

"Many explorers have died searching for the Lost City of Gold, including Percy Harrison Fawcett and his son, the inspiration for *Indiana Jones*." They disappeared under unknown circumstances during an expedition to find 'Z'—Percy's name for the ancient city.

"There was another group, a French American expedition in 1971, led by Bob Nichols, Serge Debru, and Georges Puel. They traveled up the Rio Pantiacolla from Shintuya in search of Paititi. The party's guides left them after their thirty-day agreement expired; the three continued on their journey but never returned.

"A Peruvian explorer Carlos Landa led many expeditions in search of Paititi. He was the one who discovered the Inca stone path located in the mountains and was the first person to document and disseminate the Hualla fortress located in the rural area of Calca. He concentrated on the plateau where he believed Paititi was located."

"Okay, this is crazy, we're heading on an expedition where most people died. Is there any scientific proof that something is really there besides a mushroom, maybe gold?" asked Luci.

"Glad you asked. Yes, a French-Peruvian couple Nicole and Herbert Cartagena, discovered the ruins of Mameria. For the first time, the researcher discovered Inca ruins in Amazonia. This discovery constitutes the first scientific proof of the presence of a mysterious civilization, there were Incan remains found in Mameria and the documentation of the petroglyphs at Pusharo," Nick answered. "In 1997, another guy, a biologist named Lars Hafskjold who set out to discover the ancient tribe of Toromona, the origins of the Paititi legend. He felt that this group of people were originally Helike survivors."

"Cool. Did he have any documentation?"

"Unfortunately not. He disappeared somewhere in the unexplored parts of Bolivia and was never seen again."

"Not helpful," Luci replied.

"No, but in 2005 Theirry Jamin and Herbert Cartagena studied Pusharo petroglyphs and discovered large geoglyphs in a valley nearby. Sarah called them, and they were willing to share their information."

"Cartagena seemed to get around. Fascinating," Luci said while looking down at her phone.

@lucidefoix, where are you, bitch?

"They found a 'map' showing where the city might be located. They were setting up more expeditions but ran out of funding. Are you okay, Luci?" Sarah queried.

Ignoring Sarah, Luci answered, "Is that why they want to help us?"

"In part, they are scientists; they do want their names on their research papers for their universities and more grant money."

"Sarah, do you recognize that man at the table to your left?"

"No, why should I?"

"I don't know, but he looks familiar."

"What the hell?"

"I recognize him," Nick said.

"I'm going to go find out right now," Luci said.

"Wait..."

***

"I traveled almost around the world, and who do I find? Let me answer, the man on the plane who bumped into my chair."

"Hello, Luci, I couldn't help but overhear your conversation. Please let me introduce you to my sister Pamela. We are staying in Cuzco. How bizarre that we are meeting up like this."

Pamela's face appeared as though someone had painted a sultry stare with thick arched eyebrows, and warm, large lips.

Luci's mind spun as she muttered, "A week ago..." She couldn't think of how to ask if he'd been following her. That was paranoid; he was merely another passenger on a flight. But she couldn't help it, "Were you follow—"

"We just happened to be on the same airplane that day," Dr. Sanchez said.

"Gregorio flew home to help me find the right place for my new discovery. We're headed for the Archeological Museum, Ms. de Foix. You're the scientist my brother has told me so much about. He told me he saw you on the plane coming here. Would you like

to see a picture of my discovery? I'm sure you'd be interested."
Pamela started to open a folder, thick with documents, but Luci
stopped her.

"Wait, I have very little time now. I need to catch up with my
sister. Let me give you my card, and we can discuss this on another
day." *Plus, I'm going to Google you to see if you're legit.*

Pamela opened her mouth to speak, but Gregorio jumped in first.
"We've stumbled on an ancient clay pot that had been under a
newly excavated site not far from my sister's home that no archeologist we've spoken to recognizes. There is writing on it, that no
one has ever seen. Something incredible, but there's a problem..."
His voice dropped as he fixed his eyes on Luci, "It could be deadly
if this information falls into the wrong hands. We're hoping you'll
help us stop that from happening."

"Maybe this is a coincidence, but while I was in Crete, I heard
some rumblings in the science community about a shard with
weird writings on it discovered in South America. If this is the
same type of writing that I have on the pot, maybe it can help us
decipher this one. You wouldn't happen to know anything about
it, would you?" Pamela said.

"I'm sorry, how did you hear of these writings?"

"I believe I overheard you and your sister speak about it just now."

"I don't think so...so what's going on here?"

"I heard you are an expert at decoding written language."

"Maybe all of this is just a coincidence, the plane, finding a clay
pot that has the same writing that is on the shard I found...You
know I did, by the way. And now you and your sister just happen
to be here, the same city that we're in. Maybe this is a just elaborate
hoax, or..."

"What are you talking about, Luci? I am one of the scientists
collaborating with your uncle," he said, frustrated.

"Really?" Luci said, curiosity getting the better of her. "But this
better be good. Let me see the pictures of your pot."

***

Xander watched the interchange between Luci and the new arriv-
als and smiled. Ivan would be pleased with this information.

March 1536

Searching around the home for her mother, Calisto's breath jumped in rapid gulps. She crept across the cobbled floor on which her Patera had built their home. Her Mitera would have escaped if she had heard the brown warriors approach.

Athena's soft melodious tone would single itself out from the crude voices of the five men. Although some of the shutters were rotting, Calisto strained to peek through the window. Three large Incans, armed with knives, and wearing wooden helmets with the insignia of their order, surrounded her mother. One wore bright feathers with a quilted cotton armor, and one of the others wore a mantle of blue.

Calisto tiptoed backward, around the rear of the house, but she bumped into something. "Oh, God!"

Calisto sighed in relief when she saw it was only a water barrel—almost empty after a miserable winter's rainfall—that stood in her way. She ducked behind it and headed towards the front door.

"My God! What do I do?"

Trembling, Calisto took shelter behind the pigsty. She watched her home for a very long time and listened for her mother.

Finally, Calisto heard. A piercing scream.

March 2, 2020

Sitting in the alcove of Cicciolina, Luci, Nick, and Sarah waited for their new friends, Gregorio and Pamela, to show them the "secret text." Luci could barely contain herself. It took her mind off the past and directed her toward the future—a long lost secret. What was the mystery? Why were people dying? She gazed around the restaurant and thought about the last time she ate—at the hotel this morning, and now she was starving.

"The city has improved quite a bit over the last years. Two of the currently acclaimed places are Cicciolina, a novo-Andean restaurant that is well established, and Baco, a relatively new wine bar and restaurant." Pamela peered around admiringly.

Gregorio stood, smiled, and looked at the hostess to let her know that everyone was now present and ready to be served.

Pamela held up a picture of the writing on the pot and handed it to Sarah. "I'm sorry, but do you know what this is?"

"It's a description of something on the pot, but the most important thing about it are the inscriptions made long ago from an island far from here."

"But, where's the mystery in that?" Luci questioned.

Pamela turned the object around in her hand, gazing at the writing and drawings. Luci wondered what other mysteries the siblings possessed.

"Pamela found this in the wreckage of a galleon of unknown origin. It's rare, and I believe from an ancient land where there was a terrible earthquake. However, what we don't know is how it got here. It has writing on the sides that no one has yet been able to identify. They suggested you might be able to help with this endeavor."

Luci turned to Pamela, who said, "My husband and I live near Lima. I was exploring the area, collecting mementos from the people who lived near the volcano, and I came across this interesting piece. It wasn't anything like my people ever made. I'm familiar with the pots, local tools, and spearheads as I'm a curator at the Cuzco museum. But this piece is far different. My husband was looking at developing the land. He wants to use the area as a tourist attraction, but we changed our minds."

"Why is that?" Sarah inquired.

"God." She made the sign of the cross. "I found a skeleton in ruins under one of the homes near what was once a water garden."

Luci frowned.

"Digging around, I found this, and a buried woman cradling it. I think the area was once used for preserving food. An archeologist heard about my find and got excited. They've started digging and found more pieces that have writing they believe belongs somewhere in Greece."

"The thing is, Luci, this discovery wasn't just the pot. I found a spear with more writing," Pamela said.

"Did you show your find to the archeologist on-site?"

Pamela gazed down at her hands that were resting on the table as if in embarrassment.

"I do not believe they were going to share the information with everyone, so I did not reveal my true find to the archeologist."

Gregorio glanced at Luci with his liquid brown eyes. "Luci. The real find seems to be the mykite."

He was attractive, Luci thought.

"And that isn't just a stone spear; it's of a material that I'm not familiar with."

"The pot has a symbol etched on the side—an Inca warrior with a headdress," Nick said.

Luci slid her finger across the etching of the symbol and cut her finger. "*Oh.*"

"Hey, are you okay?" Gregorio asked.

She moved her finger on the inside portion of the shard, and the small cut began to close up.

Startled, she clutched her cell as it beeped.

@lucidefoix you'll die soon

***

"First, let me tell you about the area around Lima where there are many hidden caves, and why we believe this might point to a Lost City."

"If you remember your history, in January 1531, Francisco Pizarro set out on an expedition to conquer the Inca Empire and landed on Puna Island. Pizarro only had 169 men and 69 horses; they headed south and occupied Tumbes, where they heard about the civil war between brothers, Huascar and Atahualpa. In September 1532, after reinforcements arrived from Spain, Pizarro founded the city of San Miguel de Piura, his men stormed into the center of the Inca Empire, with again, remember 106 foot-soldiers and now 62 horsemen. Atahualpa , the Spaniards took advantage of the brothers' war. Pizarro marched into Cajamarca with his army of 80,000 troops, which were mainly Incans whom he had convinced to join him. Atahualpa heard that this strange group of men was advancing into the empire, and he sent an Inca nobleman to investigate. The man stayed for two days in the Spanish camp, assessing the Spaniards' weapons and horses. Atahualpa decided that the 168 Spaniards weren't a threat, so he invited them to visit Cajamarca, expecting to capture the Spaniards. Pizarro and his men advanced unopposed through challenging terrain and finally arrived in November 1532."

"How about if we cut to the chase. Where's the gold?" Nick asked.

Ignoring Nick, he continued, "After they killed Atahualpa and most of his men, some escaped to Cuzco. That is where many believe the Lost City, with its seven caves of gold, is located. They were sent there to protect the area from the Spaniards. Many good men have already traveled in that direction and have lost their lives. It's a fool's journey, Luci."

"Yet, you'd like to go?"

"Yes, I think our expedition should keep in touch with you. We'd go separate ways so that we can cover more ground. What do you think?"

"I think there is safety in numbers, so yes, I think it's a good idea. What do you think, Sarah and Nick?"

"I've had contact with Gregorio before in Helike. He was invaluable on the expedition, so I believe he would be an asset." Sarah looked at Luci pensively as if to say, *but can we trust him?*

"I'll reserve judgment on this until later," Nick added.

Gregorio lifted his eyebrow as if this was a challenge. "Thank you for this opportunity. Now, my dear sister, let's get you home. Tomorrow is a big day for me."

"Aren't I coming on the trip?"

"No *quierdo*, you'll be best here, setting up materials to be delivered later to us."

She sighed dejectedly. "As you wish."

March 3, 2020

The next morning they found themselves with the expedition team outside the hotel with ten men and five jeeps. Gregorio joined his group of five at the hotel. Luci watched as Max pulled up and began talking privately to Nick, then jumped into a Jeep with his backpack.

They spent seven hours on the road. As they began their ascent into the jungle, Luci glanced over at the GPS: 10,000 feet above sea level. They pulled over to set up camp where Sarah and Luci watched a fantastic red sunset over a mountain pass. Luci reached for her camera inside the backpack and snapped pictures. She felt dizzy; her mind was unable to process any thought other than a sensation of panic. At one point, she felt she was drowning. Her mind went into overdrive, her first thoughts were of Max, Nick, and Sarah...her family. Luci wondered if they were going to find the Lost City without any in the group dying.

***

"Where are you?" Ivan screamed.

"Lima, Peru. That's where Sarah was headed. I'm not far from their hotel," said Xander.

"I've ordered a jet with a crew of local mercenaries to meet up with you."

"What do we do about Max?"

"I heard he was injured at the Vatican. I doubt he'll be much trouble, but if he is...kill him."

***

"Wake up."

Luci sleepily opened her eyes to see Max standing above her. Darkness and power seeped out of him.

"Come on; we've got to go now, I hear movement," Max impatiently said. He shut the tent opening and ran off to warn others.

What are you doing here? was all Luci could think as she tiredly picked herself up, threw her clothes in a bag, and raced to warn Sarah, of what she wasn't sure. "Someone is here. I don't know how we were tracked, but Max is barking orders at everyone. Sarah, we need to evacuate quickly."

In the distance, she heard the sound of a drone. Low, coming over the water from the west.

Shit.

***

@lucidefoix I'm getting closer to you and your friends, kiss them good-bye

March 4, 2020

Luci could see the blue lights of the drone coming straight toward them. The muscles of her stomach clenched. *Don't be sick. Take a deep breath. Breathe.*

"We have to get away from here, Luci," Sarah said. "The Russians will go to any length to capture you. They need you to decipher the last piece of the puzzle. I'll go with Nick, Gregorio, and the team, you go with Max and Alexy. We need to split away from each other. Besides, with smaller numbers, we'll move more quickly and make it difficult for Ivan to find us. Look at these GPS coordinates. Meet up with us here at Devils Falls." Sarah pointed to a map. "It's by a lake shaped like a figure eight."

Luci heard a sound from behind the tent and whirled around in that direction. Max was coming toward her. His expression...

Luci instinctively lifted the gun in her hand.

"Good, you have a gun."

"I like to be prepared after our last foray in Italy."

"Give me the gun, unless you've learned how to use it."

"Point and shoot, right?"

"Yes, but it's the accuracy that matters. Now give me the gun."

Luci didn't move.

"Give it to me. We need to get out of here. Besides the Russians, it could be drug traffickers, illegal loggers, or miners. These groups are overtaking this part of Peru, and many archeologists, explorers, or just people taking a hike are killed."

"The Russians are close, I can feel it. We have protection here, Max," Luci said.

"Not enough. There may be several of them. They'll expect to mow everyone down and snatch you away. I'm not letting that happen."

"Stay and help me end this now, so we're free to search for a valley that hides the Golden Caves."

"When did you find that out, Luci?"

"At the restaurant. Gregorio allowed me to take pictures of his shard. I was able to piece together clues while using the shards we have in our possession. I know approximately where we need to go, but I need more time."

We don't have any time; these men are out to kill me and take you.

"We pick our battles, and in this one, we would lose." He reached out and knocked the gun from her hand.

"Dammit!" she screamed.

He muttered a curse as she dived for her gun.

An agonizing pain shot through the back of her neck.

Darkness.

She was rudely awakened by her body being jostled along. Luci opened her eyes to discover she was being carried on Max's shoulders. "Max put me down, this hurts. What did you do to me?"

"Stop moving, or I'll drop you. And be quiet, men are searching for us."

"Let-me-down," she snarled.

***

Over the next week, the rough and overgrown trails continued downward through the increasingly broken and precipitous territory of the Valley of Iacco. It was easier to follow the river itself with its raging waters and substantial slippery boulders and logs than to support the overgrown and uprooted remnant of a trail clinging to the valley wall a few hundred feet above.

"Are we headed in the right direction, Max? We need to find a lake."

"We're getting close; I see some ruins up ahead. Let's take a breather; this altitude is getting to me."

"Are you sure it's safe?"

"Nothing here is safe, but I think we'll find somewhere to hide within the ruins up ahead. And I'm getting soaked in this downpour. Will it ever end?"

"Yeah, I could use a change of clothing. I'm cold and wet."

Cautiously walking toward the Incan ancient ruins through the isolated tropical range, Luci caught a glimpse of the mighty peaks of an isolated massif, which seemed to reach a height uncommon for these tropical mountains. A thick mantle of green vegetation was shrouded in perpetual clouds around the summit that harbored extensive stone ruins.

Entering the Iacco labyrinth and following original Incan stone paths, their guides told them of a remote mountain. At its top was supposedly an old stone city.

"I wonder if this could be where the caves of gold are located." Max peered at the unusual formation above them.

"I'm not sure, but I think there are many Incan cities yet to be discovered. Let's sit for a while. Wait, just up ahead, there is an unusual—check that—unique geological formation I want to examine. It's called a diatreme."

"What's that?" Max asked.

"It's a volcanic formation in which magma deep in the earth rises toward the surface, encounters an underground body of water, and essentially explodes. It creates water connected to a volcanic pipe below highly fractured rock," Luci said, her fears gone and her knowledge taking over.

"Can you call Sarah? See if she's made it to the lake with her group?"

"I see men running towards us. We've got to get out of here."

"What if it's Sarah?" Luci said, worriedly.

A bullet shattered the rock right next to Luci.

"Holy shit, who are these men?"

They spun around in the opposite direction heading for the old stone city.

"He doesn't want you dead, Luci, but he sure as hell doesn't give a shit about me."

"I don't want you dead," another bullet whizzed just past her, right next to where Max was running, a man with an accent said.

"Keep your head down; there is a swarm of tarantulas ahead," he screamed at her and Alexy.

Luci ducked as far as she could without tripping. Sure enough, there was the mother of all tarantulas just above her. "Shit, shit, shit."

***

A man in dirty, tattered clothing stepped around Luci and rushed at Max. A second attacker stepped on a stick lying near the path. The little piece of wood snapped, and Max spun around to find Luci being held hostage while another guy was charging Max's way.

He aimed his gun at the second man's chest and readied himself to pull the trigger.

"Put the gun down." The man holding Luci spoke in perfect, accented English. His mouth and nose were covered with a red kerchief.

Max didn't move. He could shoot the guy who'd frozen in mid-attack, but then the man holding Luci could quickly end her life. Then there was the difficulty of the three other men in the group, all pointing weapons at Max and Alexy.

With no wiggle room, Max nodded and eased the rifle strap over his head and shoulder, dropping it on top of the weapon before standing up straight and putting his hands in the air. He nodded at Alexy to do the same.

"The pistol," the man in charge ordered.

Max grunted and did as he was told, removing his sidearm from its holster and placing it next to the rifle.

"And now the machete."

Max sighed and tossed the blade on the ground. "Anything else?" he asked in a tone layered with disgust at himself for allowing these men to get the drop on them.

"Is there anything else I should know about?"

"I have ammo in my backpack."

"Thank you. Set it on the ground as well."

"What are you doing in my jungle?" he asked. "This is no place for a woman and white men." The man's Spanish accent was refined and smooth. He most definitely had not been raised in the jungle.

Two of the other men pushed Luci toward Max.

"Sightseeing." We own a travel agency for intrepid explorers who are interested in finding the Lost City of Gold."

Luci shot Max an irritated glance.

"Hey, you know the jungle well. Would you like to be one of our guides? We could pay you well."

The leader laughed. "You're a funny guy. I have to say, your response is both original and humorous." He raised his pistol and pointed it at Max. "Now tell me why you're here. My first guess is that you're drug enforcement. The problem with that is the lady is not armed, and there is no jurisdiction out here."

"We're not with any agency," Max said. "Well, she is…she runs an archeological agency."

Luci scowled at Max.

"Relax, Luci, these guys don't care what we're looking for."

The leader was piqued. "Well, what are you looking for, gold?"

"It's nothing," Luci said.

"We brought these guns because we heard there are animals and a band of rebels out here. And, Alexy, you really are a lousy bodyguard."

The man in charge cocked his head to the side and gave them a skeptical glare. "Do you expect me to believe that two men and a woman were out traipsing around the jungle looking for gold? Do you think I'm stupid, gringo?"

"No, no sir, we don't think you're stupid," Luci chimed in.

"Then, who are you? Are you spying on my operation for another cartel? If you're not with any government, then that must be the answer, and if that is the answer, you're going to die."

A tarantula dropped from her web and landed on one of the men. Terrified, the man screamed, and in the chaos of men running around trying to kill the spider without killing their comrade, Luci, Alexy, and Max made their escape.

***

Luci glanced down at the map. Cool mist poured over her and Max as they shuffled their feet sideways on a narrow shelf toward the back of the waterfall to meet up with the other members of their party. "It reminds me of the underground cavern we were chased into without the water."

"How could I forget! We found the burial site of *Esclarmonde and the lost codex,*" Max said.

They broke out their flashlights from the backpacks and played the beams off the water in the pool below their feet. "Do you think this is where the Golden Cave is?"

The crashing sound of the waterfall was overwhelming and only grew louder with every step. They kept moving, an inch or two at a time with their heels hanging over the narrow ledge, their hands pressed firmly against the wet rock wall.

"No, it's quite a way from here."

Luci's nose was pressed against the rock wall; she prayed the whole time that she didn't slip into the water. Max disappeared behind the falling white water.

Luci followed. The narrow edge turned into a full landing with a shallow cavity cut into the rock. That is where they spied Sarah, Nick, Gregorio, and the rest of their group. At the same time, Alexy stayed outside guarding the cave entrance.

The ground was wet, mist billowed away from them. "I've never been so happy to see someone," Luci exclaimed.

Sarah leaped up and hugged Luci. "Let's get you into some warm clothes. You're sopping wet."

Luci looked around at all the men. "Ahh, where?"

Sarah smiled. "Just around the bend, there is another alcove. We can have some privacy there." Sarah led the way into an alcove hidden by stalactites. "Much better?"

"Yes, thank you." Luci grabbed a sweater and jeans out of her pack. "How's it been here?"

"There haven't been any problems, you?"

"We were chased by drug dealers, but we got away. I don't think they've followed us."

"It's been pretty boring here. We arrived three hours ago. We ate—speaking of which, have you eaten anything?"

"No, not much. It would be nice to get warm and eat something. Can we build a fire in here?" Luci asked.

"I really don't think it's safe. Carbon monoxide poisoning could happen in this little space," Sarah answered.

"Ssssh, do you hear that?" Max peered around the alcove.

"No, what?" Luci whispered.

"I heard a sound, like a gun going off."

"How could you hear that with the roar of the waterfall? My ears are still ringing," Luci said.

"Stay here, I'm going to take a peek. Don't say anything, and don't move."

***

Rodrigo and his men made it onto the landing just outside of the waterfall and stopped for a second to look around. "Can you see anyone?" Rodrigo asked.

"Hell, I can't see or hear anything." Xander continued his search around the alcove with his gun drawn. Xander had happened upon Rodrigo while following Luci's trail and offered him a hefty sum of money when he discovered that they knew where Max and Luci were headed.

Rodrigo yelled something to his men, but the archeological group couldn't hear much of anything. The drug runners kept moving until they were right on the group and surprised them.

"Ahh, it looks like we found what we were looking for. Hello Max. Introduce us to your friends," Xander said.

Max looked up, sullenly at his pursuer. "We are archeologists looking for a lost city. We told you this before."

"Where is my little Luci?" Xander inquired.

"I left her behind. She twisted her ankle."

"That wasn't the most honorable thing a man should do. You should have stayed with her and made our job much easier. I think I should kill you; this would give me great satisfaction considering you've wasted my time," Rodrigo said, peering around the cave.

"You could, but then where would the fun be in that? Frankly, I'm getting a little tired of your attitude, Rodrigo."

Rodrigo stepped menacingly closer, pointed the gun directly at Max's head, then turned the gun and shot one of Max's guides.

"That will be enough!" Xander threatened.

***

Sarah sneaked back to Luci. "There are men in the alcove. One sounds like Xander. Could be you didn't lose your drug friends after all."

"Shit, shit, shit!" Luci looked up the rock wall to an indentation in the stone. Above were two smaller cavities.

Noticing what Luci was looking at, Sarah exclaimed, "No, Luci, I can't do that climb."

Luci searched for grips so she could scale the wall. The stone, however, was wet and slippery. Grabbing a rope out of her backpack, she decided to do the climb. She had scaled a few walls at the gym before and so had a little climbing experience. She made it up to the top in less than six minutes.

Sarah gazed up dejectedly. "Throw the rope down; I think I can make it on my own."

"Let me find something to attach it to." Luci was gone for a few minutes, her light dancing around on the outer edge of the entrance.

Sarah hoisted herself up to the rocks, one foot- and one hand-hold at a time. "Did you find anything?"

"Save your breath, and yes, some interesting markings and even some skeletons."

"Let me see." Sarah was at the top peeking over the edge. Her eyes widened at the sight of a skeleton to her right.

Luci chuckled at her reaction. It appeared to be crawling out of the water, the legs buried in the sand, the arms thrown forward, skull face down. Another skeleton lay behind it, and another. As they progressed, the flat sandy cavern was dotted with skulls, rib cages, and bones.

"I'd like to take a closer look after you get all the way up." Luci lay on the ledge and pulled Sarah the rest of the way.

"I don't want to do that again."

"Going down should be much easier," Luci said.

"Easy for you to say. Where are the guys? I hope they're okay."

"I think they were smart and helped lead those men away from here. It'll give me time to decipher the markings on the wall."

"*Look*, I found a message regarding a passage that will get us out of here. I can feel the air coming out of a vent up ahead. Can you feel it?" Luci asked.

"Yes, I feel the coolness on my skin, but what about the guys?"

"Leave a cryptic note on the wall that they will only understand. They will follow."

"Do you know where we're headed?"

"I think I have a pretty good idea, there's a waterfall up ahead."
Luci moved her fingers along the writings on the wall.

"Do you know what language that is?"

"Greek with a hint of Phoenician."

"They were great shipbuilders. No wonder they were able to
make it across the Atlantic."

"Wait, shhh. Did you hear something?"

"I heard a gun go off."

"Let's get out of here; head toward the cool air."

***

"You said there is gold here, and the gringo mentioned a Lost City
of Gold," the drug smuggler said to Xander while waving his gun
at Max and Nick. "I think you're stalling for time, that's what I
think."

"You think?" Max said without thinking.

Rodrigo wasn't quite sure what he meant, so he ignored him.
"No one is coming to rescue you, my friends. So, tell us where the
treasure is before I shoot another one of you. Which one of you
would like to be the next to die?"

Max didn't have to think too long about that comment. "Let's
climb up to that ledge. We were able to decipher part of the shard,
and I hear there is a ruined temple where the gold is hidden. Many
archeologists have gone in search of it and died, but this shouldn't
be news to you." He pointed to where Luci had gone.

The men climbed the slippery rocks. One of the smugglers in his
haste slipped over the side and down to the cavern below. The men
stood looking at where their comrade had gone, their eyes filled
with uncertainty.

The drug smuggler wasn't stupid; he had the look of someone
who had grown up in the streets. "I asked you two if the treasure
was here, and you told me that it was."

"Not sure. We haven't been here before; we're only guessing.
Let's go up and see if there is any writing on the cave walls before
you shoot anyone else, and then none of us have the treasure."

***

"Where are we, Luci?"

"I think we've crawled through the cave into a hidden room," Luci replied.

"It's like time has never touched this place. Are we inside a volcano?"

"That's what it looks like to me, but it doesn't seem like it's been active for hundreds of years. Most are dormant in Peru. It's called a composite volcano."

"Meaning?"

"It's been created from years and years of eruptions and cooling, which has added layers that form the cone shapes you see above."

"What about the internal vents, and why have you stopped moving?"

"Shhh! I'm listening. I hear voices. One is Max's, and he's headed this way."

"We need to keep moving…But doesn't magma rise from those internal vents?"

"Yes, I'm certainly feeling the heat, but like I said, it's dormant."

"Has anyone seen the inside of a volcano?"

"A few." Luci shrugged.

"Are they alive?"

Luci smiled. "Look up ahead, there's an opening."

"Could it be a vent?"

"It's possible, and we can crawl right out of here."

"I hope so. Either way, we don't have much choice, but should we stay and wait for Max or leave and see what's on the other side?"

***

Max, Nick, Xander, Gregorio, the drug smuggler, and four of his party began the slow process of scaling the wall that Luci and Sarah had just climbed. At least Max sure hoped they had.

"Let's keep going. I hear a waterfall up ahead," Max said.

"If I didn't know any better, my friend, I'd think you were leading me into a trap of some kind," Rodrigo said.

"You've got to be kidding," Nick said. "You hold all the guns, you have men. We've got nothing, not even our backpacks."

"Climb up here with us," Max said. "We'll show you what we've found. Nothing."

"Look, I'm a scientist here, I don't want any trouble. I'm trying to get my name and organization on a document of scientific study," Gregorio said.

Max shot him a look of disapproval.

Rodrigo thought about it for a minute, then decided. "Okay, I'll climb up." Turning to his men, he added, "Keep your guns trained on them while I climb."

Rodrigo stuffed his gun in the holster and reached up to the first ledge. Just above ten feet high, he stopped looking back at the onlookers and focused exclusively on each hand- and foot-hold. He reached the top ledge and slapped his hand onto the wet landing, relieved to be done with the tiring climb. Nick reached over and gave him a pull-up.

Rodrigo stood up and quickly moved away from the edge, the fear of heights doing its best to make him crazy. He looked into the recess but couldn't see what the men had found since it was nearly pitch dark.

Two of Rodrigo's men shone their lights into the back, pointing at something in the corner.

"It's there," Max said in Spanish.

"According to my men, there are more symbols," Rodrigo said.

"Yes. May we proceed?" Nick asked.

Rodrigo motioned his gun for his men to follow Max and Nick and to keep an eye on them. As the other eight made their way back to the rear of the little cave, Rodrigo stole a glance over the edge and caught his breath.

The dome-shaped cavern only went back about thirty feet, more or less. Centuries ago, it may have been used as a shelter by some of the locals, although with so much mist floating in from the falls, it would have been challenging to keep their food dry.

As they ventured further back into the cave, they all had to bend down a little to keep from hitting their heads on the ceiling.

Max tilted his head to the side and looked up at the rock where the guards were shining their lights. He looked again at the strange symbols and hoped that Luci knew what they meant. Then he noticed small writing pointing to what seemed like an opening, a vent of some kind that was further ahead.

"Hey, can one of you take some pictures with your phone, or my phone that you now have?"

Rodrigo grabbed Max's cell phone out of the backpack and handed it to him. "You can take a picture here?"

Max snapped pictures of the hieroglyphics and carvings. "Maybe there is more up ahead."

Rodrigo sighed and relented, "Now what?"

Max hoped that he had given Luci and Sarah enough time to find safety.

March 1536

With her mother's scream ringing in her ears, Calisto bolted out of her hiding place, raced to the front door, and peered inside. The three warriors sat at the kitchen table, eating the stew that was meant for their evening meal.

Despite the warmth of the fire emanating out of the fireplace, a half-naked man had draped her mother's blanket over himself. Calisto's eyes widened at the sight of her mother in a crumpled heap at the man's feet.

For a split second, Calisto's breathing suspended. She burst into the room and rushed at the man sitting next to Athena. "What have you done to my Mitera?"

"Who the hell are you?" the feathered warrior asked.

Calisto fell at her mother's side. A terrible, acrid smell similar to burnt meat, caught in her nose.

Her mother's eyes flashed with determination as she whispered, "Don't tell them who you are."

Her mother's face was streaked with blood where a knife had cut into the skin on her forehead.

"Is this your son?" The leather-clad Incan pushed his foot between her mother's legs.

Then he swung around and kicked Calisto in the stomach. She clutched her sides, the breath knocked out of her. Muscle spasms rocked through her making her swoon. She squeezed her eyes shut tightly against the ache in her stomach and struggled to catch her breath. After a few minutes, she gasped, "Why are you doing this?"

"She is a Tlahuelpuchi and must die," one of them said.

"No! My mother delivers babies. She does nothing but help the people outside our village."

"Shut up!"

"There is a sign of witchcraft here." He pointed to her mother's basket. "I see potions and medicine. And there is a goat outside to sacrifice."

Calisto wiped the back of her hand across her sweating forehead; her cap fell off and revealed her long, blonde locks.

"Aha! A young woman dressed as a man." Another warrior sucked the stew's juices off his fingers. "So, you must be the heretic, Calisto Cristobal."

Calisto stared at him. How did he know who she was?

March 11, 2020

"Did you hear that?" Luci quietly asked.

"Yes, I hear Nick and Max's voices, but there are others with them."

"Yeah, that's what makes me nervous. I can't hear Xander's voice, and Alexy is either gone, or he's out looking for us."

"I think we need to keep going," Sarah said. "But now I'm really terrified."

Slowly, they lowered their feet over the edge and started the arduous climb down toward the back of the cave. The wet rocks from the waterfall made it harder going down than going up. It was also much more difficult finding the right places to grab or place a toe, and the light in the distance wasn't helping a great deal.

Luci's boot hit the ground. She let out a breath of relief. Sarah touched down immediately after her, and the two women stepped back away from the wall.

They had a growing concern about where they were. What was happening with Max and Nick swelled in Luci's mind with every passing second.

Was it the cartel? Or was it someone else...the Russians? Perhaps it was another scientific expedition just like them.

Luci shook off the thoughts and flicked her head toward Sarah. "Let's find a hiding place and wait for Max and Nick, and whoever else they're with."

They scurried ahead and hid behind some boulders waiting and watching, never suspecting that others were watching them.

***

Rodrigo waved with his pistol to the men. "Nice and slow," he said. "or one of you will die."

Max and Nick glanced at each other knowingly. Max knew they had to outsmart this drug smuggler, or God knew what would happen to them.

They moved in tandem toward an opening in the back of the cave. A brilliant light showed through, fresh air wafted across Max's face. He shifted uneasily in the small enclosure, then fell in line behind one of the smugglers as the man led the way out. One of Rodrigo's men lay face down below the edge on which they were treading.

"I hope, *señor*, this is not your doing." Rodrigo walked onto the ledge behind the last of his guards.

The first to exit the cave pointed a gun at Max, who was focused exclusively on the rock formation. He thought he had caught a glimpse of Luci. One by one, the men traversed the slick, black rocks until they were all safe on the other side of the volcano.

The guards under Rodrigo's orders made camp on the ledge. Suddenly another of Rodrigo's men fell back with a bullet in the center of his head.

Max, Gregorio, and Nick knew this was their chance; Alexy had come through for them. They'd been waiting for the opportunity to present itself. Now they'd received their wish.

Rodrigo walked over to his dead comrade, losing focus. "Someone else is in this cave. Do you two know what happened?"

As one, Max, Gregorio, and Nick ran toward the opening, hoping that Alexy wouldn't miss and accidentally shoot them.

A weapon glinted in the light. Max hit the ground, fearful he might be shot. Two other men weren't as lucky. Gunfire erupted all around the cave; bullets tore into chests, legs, and arms.

Max looked up; the two other gunmen had fallen over the ledge, faces empty of life.

Nick pushed himself off the ground, but the right side of his jaw met the top of a boot. Dull pain shot through Nick's face as he rolled through the dirt and came to a stop in a shallow depression in the ground.

Rodrigo walked toward him, gun still in his left hand. He ran his fingers over the cut under his eye, looking at the blood as it poured out. Nick struggled to get up. This time, Rodrigo drove the tip of his boot into Nick's ribs—then again in his abdomen.

Each blow was worse than the last one. He tried to roll away, but Rodrigo was having none of it. "You're going to die." His finger tensed on the trigger.

"No!" Rodrigo screamed. He shuddered and turned toward Max with a confused, horrified look on his face. He didn't know what the guy was doing until he got up from the ground and faced him.

Then Nick saw the blood oozing out of Rodrigo's chest.

Gregorio had shot him through the back. He was dead before he hit the ground.

Max jumped up and ran over to Nick and helped him sit. Nick leaned over and put his hands on his knees for a second, catching his breath.

"Do you know who fired the guns that killed the guards?"

"Maybe the Russian climbed up the cave wall and waited for their moment." He shrugged. "Let's get out of here before they do the same to us."

"Come on, we really have to get out of here before we continue to be picked off," Gregorio said.

"Did anyone see where the Russian went?" Nick asked.

***

Luci heard guns blasting away in the caves and sprinted toward the entrance just as Max and Nick were running out.

Max spotted them coming from behind a forty-storey rock formation and waved them away.

Turning swiftly, Luci and Sarah ran away, heading deeper into a nearby brush.

"What's happening—who are those men?" Luci shouted.

"Xander didn't play nice with Rodrigo and his men."

"What do you mean?" Sarah asked.

"I don't think Ivan and his friends want to share with the cartel," Nick answered.

"Let's just keep going. There's got to be something ahead, right?"

"This is an incredible place. It's a whole new world, with rock formations, a beach, forty-storey rock quarries created at least 4-5 million years ago," Luci exclaimed.

The light coming through behind the rock hid another cave. They made their way into the cave, then walked outside where they were in the rainforest with breathtaking rock walls five miles long, *a whole week to walk through this skyscraper.*

Max, Nick, Sarah, Luci, Alexy, and the others hurried along the ridge, cutting through brush, dangling branches, and walking between hills. They proceeded up an alluvial fan into a dry wash that wound itself amongst gigantic piles of split boulders pockmarked with holes.

"Interesting terrain," Max said. "Very dramatic. These green hills, and just on the other side, a swift-moving river that stretches out between the mountains."

As far as the Americans were concerned, they couldn't move fast enough.

On the hillside across the river, a column of smoke rose from the rainforest canopy. Max stopped in his tracks to get a closer look. The others stayed behind him and gazed into the wilderness.

"Who do you think that is?" questioned Nick.

"Possibly guerillas looking for Rodrigo and his men."

Max sat on a rock and wiped his forehead with the bottom of his shirt. They hadn't had any water since early that morning, and his mouth was dry as the Sahara Desert. The humidity in the cave had pushed their bodies to the limit. Sweat rolled off his forehead and soaked his clothes.

"What I wouldn't give to take a dip in that river," Sarah said.

"I'll second that except we don't know exactly what's *in* that river," Luci said.

"Let's just stay here until nightfall, then we'll test the river, see if we can drink it and fill our canteens," Max offered.

***

A storm was approaching. Thunder boomed, and the first drops of rain spattered around them as they walked toward the river.

"Where do we go from here?" Luci asked.

"We can't go back. Xander may have enlisted more men to find us, so I guess we move forward," Max said.

"We don't seem to have any good choices," Sarah said, apprehensively.

Finally, they came around a bend in the hills only to pause at a picturesque sight: in a round valley at the base of a black ridge of lava, stood an egret ascending from the sand. Nearby, a maze of adobe walls rose above drifts of sand amid a scattering of thorny acacia.

"We can rest a bit and get out of the rain. We can start back up again after a quick nap," Nick suggested.

"Good idea. I'll keep the first watch," Max said. No one bothered to argue; they were too tired.

"How old do you guess those caves are?" Max asked.

"Maybe 4-5 million years," Luci answered.

"I don't think anyone has been here in a very long time. The caves aren't visible from the sky or from the ground. They have been covered by the canopy of trees for hundreds of years. Look, there's a stone wall where a panel of rock art of sheep and goats, with lines and triangles. The images on large boulders all decorated with mysterious geometric designs." Luci touched the stone with her fingertips. "Sarah, can you take a picture of this?"

"These designs could possibly be a map."

"The Incans had gold, but what if there is something else?"

"What do you mean, Luci?" Nick asked.

"I don't know, it just seems something that is so well hidden for thousands of years by these ancient people wouldn't be gold. It should be something more important, worth making sure that it was hidden."

"It's possible that whatever is down the road could kill us. But what if Luci's right—what if it's something that could help the world? By going forward, we could make a difference."

"Do you have any cell reception down here?"

"No, we're on our own," Luci said. *Thank God for that, at least I won't receive threatening text messages.*

***

"Hi, I was just about to call you," Xander said into his comsat military-issued phone. "We were able to dispose of the drug runners who were after our intrepid group of adventurers. We have an idea where they went after escaping from the cavern."

"It looks like they've already made a connection," Ivan said coldly. "Have you got rid of Max?"

"I couldn't at the moment we spotted him, dammit."

"Do you know where they are exactly?"

"No, I'm not familiar with the area."

"Figure it out. Prove your worth. Dispose of the men and retrieve Luci and Sarah in the safest of ways."

Cold, arrogant bitch, Ivan thought, as he hung up. He was tempted to go after the gold himself and ignore the bitch. He didn't want anything to happen to Luci before he could get his hands on her and Sarah. Couldn't forget, dear Sarah. He reached for his phone and dialed Sergei. "Get the plane ready."

"Okay, I thought I'd—"

"Shut up and just do it. Now. Have the plane ready. I might need to take off for Peru urgently."

March 12, 2020

"Do we descend this mountain?" Luci asked.

"I don't see any other way," Max responded.

Luci started down, picking her way among the razor-sharp lava rocks. Max's cracked hands were bleeding. His arms trembled uncontrollably, and waves of dizziness swept over him.

The canyon bottom was hot as an oven and filled with split boulders that had fallen from above. They scrambled over the rocks up to the far side, making only a few hundred yards over the next hour. At last, they came to a pour-over, a lip of stone fifteen feet overhead that they could neither see beyond nor get over.

"I think we need to backtrack, Max," Sarah said.

Wearily they descended the few hundred yards they had spent the past hour climbing. From there, they ascended another slope to traverse a narrow layer of rock that formed a kind of shelf above the ravine. Around a turn in the canyon, the shelf led toward the upper part of the gorge, building into what looked like a natural trail.

They inched forward on the trail, the chasm was so narrow they had to brace themselves against both sides with their arms. Luci went through the thin opening. Nick followed, overwhelmed by the scent of water.

The valley opened into a belly-like hollow of stone a hundred yards long and perhaps fifty feet wide. A mass of vines hung down a section of cliff.

"Water!" Luci said. "Just ahead. We can make camp there."

Overwhelming exhaustion fell upon the group. Clearly, they all felt the same way. They stretched out on the dark ground and fell into a deep sleep.

Luci woke and sat up in darkness. At first, she thought the evening had fallen but then realized that they had all slept straight through the night and that dawn was just breaking. Max was awake as well and looking at the diary of the missionary sent with Pizzaro. Sarah, Nick, Gregorio, and what men they had left, were still sleeping.

The upper rim of the canyon glowed gold with the rising sun, and a crisp, delicious flow of air washed over them. She looked around, taking in their surroundings for the first time.

Max seated himself next to Luci. "So, this is Shangri la, huh?"

"I'm looking to see if I can get a sense as to what direction we've come," Luci said.

"I think it's time we talk about what happened."

She knew what he was implying. "Not now, maybe never. I just don't have the energy."

"This isn't quite what it was stacked up to be."

"You mean us?" she asked dejectedly.

Nick sat up, rubbing his eyes and stretching. "Do we have anything left of the food?"

"Yeah, I have some energy bars in my backpack. I'll get some out for everyone," Max said.

"Maybe there's more canyon farther on," answered Luci. Anticipation was overcoming her hunger.

"Looks like another dead end to me," Max said.

Sarah set off along the sandy bottom of the valley, still cloaked in the shade of dawn. Luci jumped up to walk with her. Max and Nick watched wordlessly.

The upper end of the valley narrowed once again, then made a turn. They came around it only to be blocked by a blank face of stone.

"Looks like this is as far as we go." Sarah gazed up at the wall—at the basalt cliffs rising on all sides. The rising sun was gliding over the mountaintops.

Max came up behind the women. "Wait. Is that a trail?"

Luci squinted upward. "Probably made by sheep coming down to the watering hole."

"If you find the golden temple of the pharaohs, let me know," Max said in a sarcastic voice.

"I'm not sure the Helikes had pharaohs," Luci smirked.

She joined Sarah climbing up the rocky slope until the animal track skirted a precarious boulder and came out above the pour-over that had stopped their progress before. Now they found themselves looking into another dry ravine that cut steeply up a high volcanic ridge. The gorge narrowed at its far end to a small crack in the earth. They climbed toward the track through which— as they approached—a strange orange glow emerged. The whole area was filled with orange mushrooms. Luci, reaching the crack first, stopped abruptly. Max came up behind her then did the same thing.

The crevice was like a doorway into another world. It suddenly opened up. Below them lay a valley, sunken in a thick mist that glowed an orange-gold in the early-morning sun. Luci saw mysterious plants hanging from the walls and flower-dotted grasslands punctuated by mounds of deep moss. Ancient fig trees mingled with sycamores and clusters of date palms graced the landscape. She could hear the echo of burbling water. The sun cleared the rim of encircling mountains; the glow brightened, and as the shadows grew shorter, ruins took shape on the far side of the valley. A row of toppled stone columns led to a pair of gigantic statues, shattered and broken; only a few feet remained of pedestals of stone.

"Oh my God," Nick said.

The four stared wordlessly at the ruins, wreathed in swirling mists.

They walked down a trail that led into the center of the valley where it fell in alongside the embankment of a stream. A trickle of water ran across a bed of fine sand overhung with convolvuluses. The air smelled of damp earth and flowers. Larks, butterflies, and swallows flitted around.

They traversed along the embankment, the mist collecting on their clothes. Not far ahead, a massive fig tree jutted out of the ground like a muscled torso, its branches heavy with fruit. They stepped up to it. Luci picked a fig from the nearest branch, soft, round and delicious. She bit into it, the juice gushing. Max, Sarah, and Nick followed her example. They were all starving.

Suddenly, Max stopped, frozen. For a moment, Luci didn't understand, but then, catching movement out of the corner of her eye, she turned to see a woman materialize out of the mist.

***

Katerina sat watching them; several men stood silently next to her. They were bareheaded with long, blond hair that fell to their shoulders. They were all dressed similarly in a long piece of red cloth wound around their bodies, one end draped over a shoulder. Each man wore a leather belt around the middle, the sheath of a dagger with a golden handle and jewels encrusted snugged tight against the stomach.

"*Amigos?*" Nick said. "*Amigos.*"

"They don't have the skin color of the Peruvians, so I don't think they speak Spanish. Try Greek."

"Why, Greek?" Sarah asked.

"If they're descendants of the Helikes, then it would be close to the Greek language, right?" Luci said.

The girl gazed in Luci's direction.

"*Philos,*" Max said. "*Philos.*"

"You're intruders. You need to leave now. I've protected the entrance to this cave for a very long time," Katerina said in perfect English.

The greetings were ignored. A heavyset man seized Max's arm and twisted it behind, and in one efficient movement, threw him face down on the ground.

Luci looked at Max worriedly but stayed silent.

"Get off of me," Max said, struggling. "There's another storm coming and it doesn't look like it's going to let up anytime soon. The quicker we can get somewhere to figure out this next part, all the better."

"You're going to need my help. There is something horrible in your path that will unleash if I do not help to shut it off," Katerina said.

"Yeah," Luci said with a hint of trepidation in her voice. "Are you sure you want to take us?"

"After I feed you, give you shelter, and let you rest for a while, you will go home. I will seal the cave entrance for good, then we will be safe."

Max stood up after eating a meal of cheese, bread and figs, then walked down the slope close behind the young woman.

"You need to be careful here on this path between the boulders," she stated.

"Why is that?" Nick asked.

"Ahh, you'll see. Just follow the path. My people and I will remain behind you and make sure you're safe."

Sarah walked forward, followed by Max, Nick, Luci, Alexy, and their men. Halfway through, the boulders started to shake and move toward them.

Luci turned quickly, noting that Katerina and her men had not followed. "It's a trap. Turn back," Luci shouted.

The earth began to rip apart, a deep chasm opened. Gregorio scrambled up the rocks but couldn't get a hand-hold and fell deep into the crevice. Luci slipped, trying to scramble out after Nick. She screamed, falling, but caught hold of a sturdy branch.

"It's okay, Luci. Just give me your hand." He held onto a piece of the boulder and knelt to grab her hand.

Luci was dangling; her grip was weakening. She looked at Nick and swung her arm up, catching his hand. Sarah and Max were on the other side.

"Hurry, Nick. The chasm looks like it's about to close."

Nick struggled to pull Luci to safety, catching her other arm. She threw her leg upward to grab the rim, and they tumbled back against the wall. They had no time to catch their breaths; the rocks were indeed closing. They watched as Alexy tripped on a boulder and fell into the crevice.

Sarah screamed and ran to help Nick and Luci, but Max held her back. "You can't help them, it could trigger another event. Come on Luci, move."

Nick and Luci practically ran the rest of the way, dodging boulders and rocks, barely making it through when the blocks of stone closed.

"Did that woman do this?"

"Better question: where is she?" Nick asked.

March 13, 2020

Luci woke slowly. At first, she didn't know where she was and opened one eye to look around. The chemical tang of newly washed floors reminded her that she had fallen asleep outside with Max, Sarah, and Nick. But how did she get here, and where was everyone else?

She got to her feet slowly, feeling groggy, like she had been drugged. She walked in the direction of the smell of food which was close by. The dark house greeted her with silence. She hated the dark and hoped Max was nearby. A blast of wind blew her inside, slamming the door behind.

Luci crept around the house, trying to get away from a shadowy figure lurking near a window, but the more she tried to get away, the slower she went.

Suddenly, she was yanked from behind. Someone with large hands threw a shirt over her head, and tugged it tighter and tighter. A large hand closed over her mouth, she coughed, struggling for air. The room began to spin, she slipped to the ground.

Luci came around with her hands and feet tied to a chair in the kitchen. The dark figure stayed in the shadows, sipping water out of a glass. For hours, her attacker taunted her. "You deserve to die, slowly," he hissed, "you're a nosy meddler, and you need to be squashed like a bug."

A loud banging on the door stopped his ranting.

With a jolt, Luci woke from her nightmare.

She sat up, sweating. Looking around, she saw Max next to her, asleep. She grabbed onto his hand.

***

"Wake up, it's daylight." Sarah rose and rubbed her back.

"I was hoping this was a dream and we were all back in our hotel room in Cuzco," Nick added.

"What I wouldn't give for a hot cup of coffee right now," Max growled.

"I have some provisions," Luci said. "Unfortunately, I wasn't the one who carried the coffee. Let me go see what I can do. Sarah, come on and help. Maybe between the two of us we can find something." Looking down at Gregorio's pack, she said, "I can't believe we lost Gregorio. That young woman didn't need to hurt us."

"Maybe she didn't. Maybe she was warning us. I'm just glad most of us survived. Mmm, I think I have something, Luci. Max, can I go through your backpack and see what we can come up with for food?" Sarah asked.

"Sure," he said.

Luci rummaged through for her phone. She had taken photographs inside the cave at the waterfall. She studied the images for a few minutes and then turned the pages of the diary until she came to the last the little book had to offer.

Inside the folds of some of the pages were notes she'd made from earlier translations along with the coded sequences they'd discovered at the site. At least she hoped they were codes. She darted her eyes back and forth as she compared the symbols to ones from before.

Max stepped from behind the rocks and came to check out what Luci was doing.

"I took some pictures of the writings and drawings that were inside the cave. Too bad I don't have any reception, or maybe we could send it back home to see if anyone can decipher it. I'm at a loss," Luci said.

"I'm not sure that's necessary. Whoever wrote that meant it to be decrypted by a human, not necessarily a computer."

Luci got up and walked over to find Sarah.

"Where are you going?" Max asked.

"To get a pen."

Sarah held out her bag. Luci reached in and grabbed a pen from the side pocket. She returned to where Max was sitting, proudly holding up her ballpoint pen and went to work on the cipher. Then she wrote on the back of one of her previous notes, putting the symbols and letters next to each other for reference.

"If I can decode this first part, getting the last sequence shouldn't be too difficult." Luci continued working.

Nick's eyes narrowed, and the skin on his forehead wrinkled. "Did you guys hear that?"

Luci looked up. "Hear what?"

Nick tilted his head to the left, eyes squinting. "There's something else," he said in a quiet tone.

Max looked up and listened. Concern washed over his face. "He's right. Someone's coming."

"Someone's coming?" Sarah asked. "Who?"

Max hurriedly helped Luci gather up her notes and the diary. "If I had to guess, I'd say the guerillas have been following us."

"Or the Russians are out for revenge," Nick said.

"Thanks for that. Yes, it could be the Russians. Either way, we have to get going," Luci said.

"Nothing is ever easy," Sarah whined, snatching up the food she had found and stuffing it into the backpack.

***

Luci frowned, confused by the information about a healing concoction that could let you live forever, and a beautiful cave of gold written by a priest in the 1500s. In a cave they had stumbled upon, Luci was hot, tired and impatiently asked Sarah, "When were you going to tell us about the mykite? It's not necessarily gold. Maybe that's why Katerina wanted us gone. Where did you find this information?"

"When I was researching the archives in France after we met up with Gregorio, I found a book called *The Healing Herbs of Peru*. It's been reproduced a few times. Scientists have taken the information and have been searching for this place."

Nick said, "We found documents and information about the Helike escaping to South America and a family who had a map of sorts that would help them. There was a person named Calisto, but she disappeared late in 1536 after her journal was published."

"So these people could all be descendants. Could Katerina be related to the Helike woman named Calisto who disappeared?"

"Seems highly unlikely, unless she's their great-great-great grandmother."

Nick turned to Luci and Max. "We have seen the journals, but we have no idea how this moss, mushroom, algae, or mykite helps the healing process. Take this woman named Calisto, who was mentioned. She concocts a potion with miraculous healing powers. She puts it all together in this secret cavern near an underground waterfall."

"Maybe this herbalist was related and passed down the information."

Nick shuffled some papers he was carrying. "I found an old book on the Inca warriors coming into villages looking for the miracle cure, raping and killing the villagers."

"If they found her, which seems likely, then maybe they thought Muri was a witch, and you know what they did to women who had healing powers back in that day."

"Heretic or witch, we need to find that magic elixir and protect it."

"What do you mean to protect it?" Luci asked.

"As you know, we're not the only ones looking for this place. It's all over the Internet; big pharmaceuticals have been trying to find it and replicate it."

"Ancient secrets bring out the crazies, including the Russians," Sarah said.

"This stuff, in the right hands, could be powerful," Max said. "Obviously, they're willing to kill for it." He looked at Sarah and Luci.

"This could be worth a lot of money, Luci, and we think people are being murdered because of it."

"What knowledge did he have?" she wondered. "Hey, I'm down for the night, I'm going to sleep."

March 1536

Grunting in pain and lying on the cold floor, Calisto refused to grab at the spasms ripping through her stomach where the Incan warrior had kicked her, instead, she focused her eyes on the naked body of her Mitera lying next to her on the cold floor slab.

Athena turned her face. Her scarf flopped to one side and fell off.

Calisto jerked back; her jaw dropped. She blinked in disbelief. Her mother's head had been shaved. Clumps of her long blonde hair lay scattered on the floor in front of the fire. "Mitera, what's happened to your hair?"

As she lifted the shaven locks, the burnt bread smell became noxious. Calisto flinched, trying to suppress the bile rising in her throat. These men had burnt her hair.

From the corner of her eye, Calisto spotted a dagger, matted with blood and hair, on the table. The sharp blade was about the length of her foot. She moved her eyes slowly around the room, checking the other warriors, but she couldn't see if they had the same lethal weapons.

The leather-clad Incan who had kicked her turned to the others. "Should we shave this little witch as well?"

He lifted his dagger and twirled it around and around. Its curved point carved a tiny hole in the wooden table that her Patera had built.

"The vampire didn't have any markings of the devil under her hair, but this one might."

They called Athena a vampire.

March 14, 2020

Jostled awake, Luci found she was being carried away from her friends by men who were dressed similarly to the Helikes, who set them up to be squashed by boulders. She screamed, but nothing came out of her mouth. She felt paralyzed.

The air grew hotter with every movement and filled with a bitter, acrid smell like sulfur. The rumbling ceased as the group continued downward into a deep recess of the cave where she had fallen asleep. The men walked cautiously, but Luci felt a deep unease in the silence. What were these men doing, and where were her friends? She struggled, but this man was too strong.

Somehow, she had to get away, at least warn her friends. She dropped her grandmother's ring near a boulder. Hopefully, they would find it, take it as a warning and leave.

After walking 150 feet or so downward, the left-hand wall cut sharply in the other direction and gave way to a dramatic drop-off. One of the men in the lead pointed his light into the abyss as if to demonstrate that trying to escape would lead to horrific consequences. He set her on her feet.

A crevice about forty feet wide dropped hundreds or more feet to the bottom where a narrow river of bright orange glowed through the pitch blackness.

Luci risked a look over the edge for a moment before taking a wary step back toward the safety of the right-hand wall. She leaned her shoulder into the stone.

"What's that gold glowy stuff?" Luci asked, not expecting an answer.

"Mykite," said the man in the lead. "Keep moving."

He understood English. They must be Helikes, like that young woman, Katerina.

They proceeded into the depths until the ramp leveled off and curved around to the right. The temperatures had to be over 100 degrees. The air was thick and difficult to breathe, full of fumes.

More Greek symbols adorned the doorposts and header, was this a warning?

They finally exited the cave and stepped onto the valley floor. Luci jumped away from the man.

***

Dizzy from lack of food and water, Luci fell to the ground and tumbled down an embankment. Katerina, with her long blonde hair, rushed towards her.

"Where did you come from?" Luci asked, dazed.

"Over there." She pointed toward the thick forest.

"You're the young woman who left us by the moving boulders. Are you Helike? Do you know where my friends are?" Luci tried to get up but screamed in pain. Blood streamed from a deep cut in her leg. The woman helped Luci lie back down on the ground.

"I tried to prevent the boulders from hurting any of you. It's a trap to keep people away from us. You're hurt. I can put medicine on your leg, and you will be well soon."

"I'm not too sure about that." Luci grimaced at the horrible smell emanating from the golden pulp.

"It doesn't smell too good, but my mother is a healer, and she takes care of all the people who live here. My name is Katerina. What is your name?"

Luci looked away as Katerina opened a deerskin bag and gently applied the salve to her deep wound. "It will be okay, you'll see."

"Luci, my name is Luci."

Off in the distance, Luci heard more people coming their way on horseback.

"It is just my people. They will carry you to the village. We will ask them to find your friends."

After the incident, Luci wasn't too sure about the reception she would get. Still, with a deep laceration to her leg, she wouldn't be able to go anywhere.

"You'll need my mother to correct your leg."

"She can do that?" Luci exclaimed, surprised.

"Yes, she is exceptional. Oh, here they come."

March 1536

Calisto shivered. So, it had happened, they called her Mitera and her blood-sucking vampires. They had cut off her Mitera's hair in search of devil markings, and now they wanted to do the same to her.

The feathered Incan stood, stretched, and yawned. "Let's make her watch us brand the witch with the metal poker."

The thought of her mother's lovely skin being branded gave Calisto the chills. Seeking comfort for the guilt billowing in her gut, Calisto stroked her Mitera's spiky hair.

The other warrior stopped playing with the dagger. He dropped it back onto the table and marched outside.

A loud burp filled the room. The leather-clad warrior stood and relieved himself against her mother's head. Calisto yanked the scarf to stop the full flow splashing on her mother. She hated how her mother lay there, unable to fight back.

"Dear Zeus!"

The stench of his urine mingled with the acrid burnt hair. Again, Calisto swallowed the sour bile that shot into her throat.

From the table, the cloaked warrior laughed and grunted, "I'll do that on her bleeding breasts when the poker is finished with her."

Calisto tightened her fists. She had to do something to save her Mitera. Using the edge of her dress, she wiped the pee off her mother's coarsely shaved head. The foul stench caught in the back of her throat, but she refused to cough and choke as her stomach heaved. She would not give these men the pleasure.

Her mother gripped Calisto's arm and yanked her closer. Her eyes were ravaged with pain and discomfort. "Promise me, Calisto."

Calisto noticed her mother had used her name for the first time. She looked into her mother's eyes and saw her sadness and heartache.

March 14, 2020

The group entered the city. Luci was carried on a gray horse to the center of the town. She didn't know what to expect, but it certainly wasn't a monolithic white temple in the background. Children raced around playing games with others outside classrooms, singing, and dancing. People strolled about, happy. To one side: an open market.

Her leg felt much better. She spotted an old lady coming towards her.

"Look, here comes my mother, her name is Calisto," Katerina said with enthusiasm.

If Luci could have melted into the crowd, she would have. This old lady didn't look very happy to see her.

"Welcome," she said through gritted teeth. "I see you've somehow managed to find your way to our home, New Helike."

"So, this is the city everyone's been looking for. Well, Calisto, I'm just happy that we all survived," Luci said.

Calisto smiled knowingly. "Not many who enter survive. Only two men I know of so far."

"So it was a test: if we lived, we got to see your home."

"Many strangers have come to our home. I survived just barely. My Mitera did not. My people found me, and we closed the cave so no one would come to our homeland ever again," Calisto said quietly.

"Why did those people do that to you?" Luci asked, curiously.

"They were warriors. They did what they were told. They thought my Mitera and I were Tlahuelpuchi…shape-shifting vampires. I did what was necessary to save myself, my family, and to preserve our way of life."

"But, we never did anything to you, Calisto."

"The people following you will do something to us as well as to you and your friends."

"How can you be sure?"

"Some men are hidden around the outside of the caves, listening, and waiting."

"For what?" Luci asked, curiously.

"For signs that let us know what they want. They desire not the knowledge of our ancient society but gold, and the mykite that was put on your leg to heal you by my daughter, Katerina." Calisto smiled down on her daughter.

"Again, we mean you no harm. We are an archeological expedition. All we want is knowledge not of gold but of you, how your people survived the crossing of the ocean and the mykite that we've read about in a diary."

"The mykite was put on your leg, and we freely give that to you."

The people of the temple gathered around Luci and Calisto, and Luci grew nervous.

"I need to get back to my friends, Calisto."

"In time, Luci. When you are completely healed."

March 15, 2020

The sun shone brightly in the encampment, and people were stirring. Max walked over to Luci's tent and lifted the flap. Looking at the bundle of blankets on the cot, he walked over and gave it a shove. No reaction. He lifted the covers. No Luci. He returned outside. "Hey, has anyone see Luci?" Max yelled out.

"No, not since last night," Nick said.

"She's probably behind those rocks over there. I'm sure she'll be here in a minute."

"Someone's coming," Max said.

"Luci?" Sarah asked.

Max tilted his head to the left to try to hear better. "There's more than one person," he said quietly.

"Who?" Nick questioned.

"If I had to make a guess, I'd say the Russians have found us."

"Or maybe some of the cartels made it and are out for revenge."

"I think we need to get out of here fast," Sarah replied.

"Find Luci," Max said.

March 1536

Calisto wanted to turn her eyes away so her Mitera wouldn't read her guilt, but her mother's eyes held her. "Say nothing of your paintings in the cave, or they will do these terrible things to you," she whispered.

Calisto's voice cracked. "Never. Our secret is safe, Mitera."

"You need to run away, go to the caves. You'll be safe there. Our people will care for you."

Calisto nodded; she'd rather die than give up their secrets. She said, "I will never give up."

The warriors continued speaking at the top of their voices, eating the stew with loud burps and grunts.

Again, Mitera took the opportunity to whisper, "I don't think it could be one of our people who told on me. But maybe—"

"Tell me, Mitera. Who told on us? I will find them and kill them."

Exhausted, she lay her shorn head back on the stone floor, looking too worn-out to say any more.

The big warrior kicked the door open with his sandalled shoes and barged back into the kitchen. Calisto stared as he inserted a poker into the fire. The flames heated the surface; on each end, two sharp U-shaped points looked pinched together.

Blood pounded in her ears.

Zeus!

March 15, 2020

Luci was taken inside a walled complex high above the city.

"It is designed to look like the form of a puma, a sacred animal to our people," Katerina said. "Over there," she pointed, "is the main plaza. A river to your left forms the spine, and the hill, its head. There are three walls built on different levels with limestone of enormous sizes. The zigzagging walls represent the teeth of the puma's head. It is built in such a way that a single sheet of paper will not fit between any of the stones."

Luci was amazed at the intricacy of the city, not to mention the complexes connected by a staircase and fountain structures. Beside the houses lay an area of agricultural terraces. Looking ahead, she saw a temple with metal-and-glass doors that opened into an enormous atrium featuring a bronze water fountain in the center portraying a sculpture of Zeus.

"This is amazing, Katerina. I can see why your mother is so protective of your homeland. I wouldn't want strangers coming here and destroying my way of life."

"I think it is more complicated than that," she answered. "I want to go out and see the world, as do many of my friends. Our elders keep us here. They say they are protecting us from the outside world. You are the first woman I have ever met, who is not from our city."

Luci was astonished. "Is that why your mother tried to trick my friends and me?"

"Possibly." Katerina furrowed her brow and looked down at the ground.

Sensing her discomfort, Luci looked away at the landscaping engineering skills, which were in strong evidence. The site's buildings, walls, terraces, and ramps reclaimed the steep mountainous terrain. They made the city blend naturally into the rock escarpments on which it was situated. A plane flying over wouldn't be able to tell people lived here.

"How many terraces are there?" Luci pointed up behind the temple.

"There are 700-terraces. I know because I counted them."

"What are they for?"

"They preserve the soil, promote our gardens, and serve as a water distribution system that conserves water."

"For being so far from the cities, and never having anyone from there, you are quite knowledgeable."

"Calisto and her family were from a faraway land, across oceans. They are highly advanced people, so my mother tells me, often."

Luci smiled. Teenagers still have issues with their parents no matter where they're from, "Ow!"

"What is wrong, Luci?"

"My leg is throbbing, I think I need to lie down and rest awhile."

"We are almost at my Mitera's home. It's inside the temple. You can rest there."

Hobbling up the stairs to the entrance of the temple, Luci saw blue and gold tapestries that dangled from the second floor on either side of several marble columns that decorated the room. The matching floor tiles covered the entire span of the area. Luci wasn't too sure about her reception. Calisto had already said others had found them but never returned. Did she have them killed? What was to stop her from doing it to her?

***

Sarah, Max, and Nick jumped behind a large boulder and spotted two horses lined up one behind the other. Like before, gunmen took aim with automatic rifles and opened fire. Bullets whizzed by.

Max spun around, yelling at the others to follow him. As he ran, he grabbed a colt 45 out of his backpack. When no one moved, he tried again, "Hey, I said follow me!"

"Have you noticed they're shooting at us!" Sarah screamed. "I'm trying not to get shot."

Nick stood up, carefully peering over the rocks and was shot in the arm by a bullet, losing his balance he toppled over the boulder to the ground.

Max jumped up, carefully squeezing the trigger one pull at a time to maximize accuracy. His weapon popped and found its target. He fired again. Another shot ricocheted off of a boulder, through a tree, and into the gunman's knee standing behind the rock. The guy grimaced and dropped to the ground.

Max couldn't see what happened from his vantage point, but he figured the bullet must have hit the guy somewhere for him to disappear so quickly.

Nick resumed his attack, recklessly spraying hot metal into the jungle behind them, occasionally hitting the mark. It only took a few seconds to empty the first magazine. He reached behind him as Sarah tossed another gun with a full complement of rounds.

"Sarah," Max ducked back behind the rocks, "hand me the other rifle."

Sarah passed the second rifle to Max. He pulled back the slide, then stuck the barrel between another set of rocks. He was about to lean out when another barrage of bullets struck the rocks beside him, sending shards everywhere, including Alexy's forehead, he never had a chance.

Max sprawled back inside for cover while the gunmen on the sorrel horses emptied their magazine. The second man wheeled around the first as the men reloaded.

Max had no intention of giving even a fraction of a second to resume the attack. He popped out from behind the boulders, locked his sights on the rider, and tensed his finger on the trigger.

Nick grabbed Max's gun, pushing it down.

"What are you doing?" Max asked, doing his best not to be angry.

Nick didn't answer. He didn't need to. Max twisted around and looked behind the first boulder. Four more men on horseback were heading straight for them with a dozen armed mercenaries.

"Oh shit," Max said.

March 1536

After several minutes of laughing amongst themselves, the big Inca with a yellow feathered headdress reached into the fire with a thickly gloved hand made of sheepskin.

Calisto's jaw dropped in horror as he lifted the metal poker and held it across her mother's naked breasts.

Her mother screamed in pain.

Calisto lunged at the warrior.

His friend jumped forward and kicked her in the stomach. Calisto doubled over, groaning in agony, and her eyes glazed as she watched the unbooted warrior lean over and lift her mother's sagging body.

He pinned her mother down with his boot in the crook of her neck. Then he glared at Calisto, his black eyes defying her to try anything.

He inserted the glowing clamps into each side of her Mitera's breasts, penetrating them with a mighty squeeze.

Her mother screamed.

And fainted.

March 15, 2020

Max and friends were marched into a camp in a river basin deep in the jungle. "What do you mean?" Max asked as he tried, with his hands bound with rope, to swat at a mosquito.

"We keep getting tracked and now caught. Do you think one of us has a GPS tracker hidden somewhere?"

"I don't know, but it's certainly something to think about. Has anyone seen Luci? Maybe she saw what was happening and got away."

A gunman behind Nick jammed him in the kidneys with the barrel of his rifle, causing the Frenchman to grimace.

"Hey, watch it. That thing could go off," Nick warned.

"This is not a good situation," Sarah said. "I wonder if they know where Luci is."

"These guys look like killers. If they caught her…" He let his words trail off.

"Well, if it's the end of the line, it's been a great ride," Max said with a smile, looking for an advantage.

"I, for one, don't share your optimism," Sarah said. "But I've always been a worrier." She giggled nervously.

"I just have a lot to live for," Nick said. "I would rather face death later as opposed to sooner."

The gunmen marched the three deeper into a camp. The procession wound its way through the outlying tents and into a central area, then left toward a considerable-sized tent covered in netting.

They passed between two guards standing on either side with automatic rifles in their hands and menacing glares on their faces. These men wore looks of unquestionable authority.

"I guess that it's probably going to be sooner than later," Max said.

"Not good," Sarah said.

The tent was dark, only a few lanterns illuminated the room. A big wooden pole in the entrance held up the original part of the roof.

"Quiet," one of the mercenaries ordered.

"Oh, so you speak English?" Nick asked.

The guy didn't answer, which made Max think maybe he only knew the one word.

Almost immediately, the man barked orders in Russian. He apparently didn't think his prisoner knew what he was saying. That, or he didn't give a shit, which seemed to be the common theme lately.

***

Luci and Katerina walked toward The Temple of the Sun—which looked like an ancient Greek building.

There were stone stairs inside the temple that they helped her to walk up. The outside was surrounded by a row of columns. Above the columns was a decorative panel of culture called a frieze. Above the frieze was a triangular-shaped area with more eruptions called pediments.

Inside the inner chamber, Luci was surrounded by statues of the God or goddess of the temple. The walls and floors were covered in sheets of gold.

Luci was dazed by all the magnificence that surrounded her, and the brilliance of Calisto dressed in a garment that draped her body. It was made from one-piece rectangles of fabric, with holes cut out for her head. The purple peplos was sleeveless, while the chiton covered part of her arms. She wore a cloak made of fine linen.

"You've entered our home. No one has entered our realm for hundreds of years. My daughter has taken pity on you and wants me to give you sanctuary. She also said your leg is broken and would like me to heal you."

"I can understand why you wouldn't want people here, Calisto, this place is amazing. We have come because my friends and I heard first about a great civilization that survived and found a diary from a priest who spoke about a healing plant that came from this area. We wanted to take a sample and study its properties so that people back home will heal quickly and be healthy," Luci said.

"Your friends will soon be brought here, but there are others who have been following you, and they want gold."

"Yes, those are dangerous men who have already done great harm."

"They know now of our home because of you and your friends. They can't be allowed to live."

Luci thought about this. "What will become of my friends and me?"

"You will live here."

"Wait. You mean forever?"

"Bring the mykite," was all Calisto said.

Perplexed, Luci asked, "Have any other people found your lands?"

"There have been a few."

"Are they alive?" Luci looked questioningly at Calisto.

"A few, the ones deemed trustworthy. The others we left for the jungle and fate. Now here's the mykite." Calisto took the plant and set to work, mashing it in a wooden bowl. The mushroom had a wondrous odor to it, almost a minty smell. Calisto took a heaped spoonful of a golden substance that looked like algae and placed the gooey substance on Luci's leg. Immediately, Luci experienced a tingling sensation in her leg. Her skin quivered, but it didn't hurt, which was odd. She took a roll of gauze from Katerina, who was standing nearby, watching what her mother was doing. She tightly wrapped the bandage around her leg.

Outside the temple, there was yelling. The noise was deafening to Luci's ears.

***

"What are you writing?" Sarah asked quietly.

"It's the code or some type of symbols that I got from the cave," Max answered.

Nick looked at the grid in the book, then the image on the paper that Max was holding.

"What have we got ourselves into?" Sarah asked.

"The thing is if this temple really does exist, and there is something inside that everyone wants a part of, and Luci is there, we better find it and fast. Right?"

"So, we're trying to find some ancient temple. Over the years, I've seen some pretty interesting stuff. You can stumble across ruins pretty frequently. But the jungle multiplies quickly, I imagine most of the ancient buildings and other structures were probably covered in a short amount of time."

"Which is why these clues are so important," Max said. "If we can pinpoint the temple's location, we can avoid needless wandering around."

"Yeah, I really don't want to do the wandering thing. But if it was so easy, others would have already found the city."

"Check."

The mercenary at the back of the tent stood up and reached into a portable table. He slipped open a drawer and removed a small box that held a note pad, a pencil, and a folded map. The man laid the stuff on the workstation. "Write down everything you've discovered about the Lost City of Gold."

"You do speak English. Good to know." Max took the pencil and paper and drew the symbols that were inside the cave while Nick held down the paper. "You know we really need to stop meeting up like this."

Xander grunted, turned away, and walked back to the corner of the room to watch, leaving behind sandwiches and water.

"It's weird," Sarah said, looking at Max. "It seems like most of those symbols circle around those three dots in the center."

"I noticed that," Nick said. "Wonder why."

Once Max had copied the symbols, he turned his attention to the notebook paper. He created a new pattern and began working through the code to translate the symbols.

Two-thirds of the way through the translation, he scowled and looked at Sarah. "This is nonsense. Just random dots and lines put together."

"Before you give up," Sarah said, "finish the code, and let's see what else it contains."

"Fine, but I'm telling you, I don't like it. Something is wrong here."

Everyone leaned in closer as Max worked, translating one symbol after another until he'd finished the entire sequence. He leaned back and put down the pencil. Max waggled his head back and forth. "I still don't get it."

"Maybe we have to shuffle the letters around to make sense of them," Sarah offered.

"No," Max said, shaking his head. "I already thought of that. There are not enough vowels to make it work."

He stood up and walked to the other side of the room to take a breath and reset his mind. He looked at the notepad, tilted his head to the side, and narrowed his eyes.

"What if—" He paused for a second to make sure he wasn't suggesting something crazy. "Maybe the answer is what's right on the ceiling of the waterfall cave. Forget the diary and the shards of pottery."

Nick stepped back toward the desk. "What do you mean?"

"Look at these images. Maybe the last site has a code all its own, a new one we have to figure out based on a completely new key."

"Then, where is the key?"

"We can't solve the thing without it."

"It's not another language, is it?" Sarah questioned.

Max stood and paced around the tent while he thought. After twenty minutes of working on it, no one could decipher the strange message. Max stretched out his arms and yawned before he moved away from the table.

***

"I'm going to take a walk if it's okay with our Russian captors," Sarah said.

She got a nod and walked out to find a place to relieve herself. Getting up from the squatting position, she looked at the sky. Twilight filled the jungle, bathing it in a paleness that grew blacker with every passing moment. The noises of wildlife died slowly, leaving the sounds of a few tropical birds to fill the air with their exotic songs.

On her walk back to the tent, a campfire crackled, sending sparks and smoke high into an opening in the canopy above. The fire's dancing tongues of orange and yellow licked the air in a wild and erratic fashion.

Sarah stared up into the sky. It was the first time she'd had a chance to relax in a while. Even though danger might lurk all around them, she allowed herself to switch off and just enjoy the sights, smells and sounds washing over her from all directions.

She hadn't had much time like that in recent memory. A few vacations with Nick were her primary conduit for rest, though those were rare. She put her palms on the back of her head and continued to gaze up into the night sky. Billions of stars twinkled like miniature lamps burning in a far-off galaxy. Others were stars in other solar systems, and a few were planets she knew well from her time spent studying astronomy.

Sarah had taken the class out of curiosity. Her major wasn't even remotely related, but that didn't matter. She'd always enjoyed looking at the stars as a young girl in the orphanage, even sitting out in the driveway to gaze up into the heavens at the incredible creation above.

She leaned back against the tent and soaked it in. Fatigue was catching up with her. As she stared into space, she tilted her head to the side. Something caught her eye. She turned her head to the other side and peered upward.

"No," she said out loud.

***

Max heard her break the silence and looked over in her direction.

"What?" Nick spoke up first. "What is it?"

Sarah swallowed and shook her head quickly. She refused her vision and stood up, still staring into the sky. They heard her, "It's too easy."

Sarah licked her lips. Her heartbeat quickened and she ran into the tent and grabbed the notepad that Max had been writing on. A few seconds later, she said, "I think I got it."

Xander perked up at the sound of Sarah's enthusiastic voice. Seeing the curious look the guard gave her, Sarah whispered, we need to escape and head out following the stars.

***

Luci looked around at the idols, stelae adorned with beautiful carvings. Some of the signs were in hieroglyphs. Outside, the area was blanketed in lush vegetation, and she found comfort in the peacefulness surrounding her. This was definitely a place she would love to stay and study. They were living memorials, more worthy than ever of investigation and study, and perhaps the only existing vestiges that could transmit to posterity the image of a Greek city.

Calisto watched as Luci admired the perfect example of the Helike style of architecture, which was characterized by lavish stone mosaics.

With the help of a cane, Luci and Calisto found themselves walking across the bridge and looking into the crystal clear water.

"The mykite...I have never seen anything like this. What is the salve made of?" Luci asked.

"It is something our forefathers brought from our homeland. We cultivated it in the caves in clay pots from Helike. I will give you a draught to soothe you and make you sleep for a short time." She scooped up the golden algae from the water's edge. "When you awake, you will be able to walk with care."

"Thank you, Calisto, I know you don't want my friends or me here, but we came looking for a lost society, one that had cures that could help all people."

"I know that now."

March 1536

The barefooted Incan lifted the bucket of water beside the fire and threw it over Mitera's wounded body. Her flesh sizzled and burnt as the warm water absorbed the heat from the red-hot tongs. Closing her eyes, Calisto tried to shut out the scene in her home.

All the memories of a mother caring for people, and healing the sick, flooded into her mind. The laughter and joy when a baby learned to walk, or a farmer caring for his family after an injury, filled her ears. The smell of Mitera's baking bread and the taste of a fresh pie filling her hungry tummy.

Calisto slowly opened her eyes. Through slits, she surveyed the kitchen, taking note of anything she could use as a weapon against these men. A flush of adrenaline tingled through her body.

Mitera moaned. More water was tossed over her. She opened her eyes and looked directly into Calisto's. The big Incan grabbed her shoulders and lifted her mother into a sitting position.

Calisto's helplessness boiled into anger. Her mother's mouth moved silently. She leaned closer in time to hear her croak, "Calisto. Promise me."

Calisto's nostrils flared. "I will never fail you, Mitera. Never!"

Suddenly, with the agility of a leopard, Calisto sprang up.

March 16, 2020

"See anything familiar?" Sarah gestured to Max's notebook and then to the stars.

"Whoa," Nick said. "I never even considered that before."

Max's eyes narrowed. "So, the symbols you found in that waterfall were actually constellations?"

"Yeah, I think Sarah got it right. See…" He indicated the drawing. "This is Vega. It's part of the Summer Triangle."

He pointed to the next drawing. "Altair?" Nick asked.

"Yep. And you can see here that it matches almost perfectly."

"And the last one?" Nick asked.

"Deneb," Sarah said. "It's a part of the Northern Cross."

Max stood up straight. "The ancient Incans and Greeks built villages, cities, and places of worship based on the stars. They studied the heavens relentlessly. Some people say they placed their buildings as mirrored locations on the planet to please the Gods. Others say they did it because of their belief in the sacred connection between earth and sky."

"One thing is clear: ancient civilizations respected the stars. They knew there was some kind of connection between what's in space and who we are. The Hopi traveled thousands of miles to build towns along with a celestial pattern. The Aztecs and Mayans similarly did their construction."

"So, you think the constellations might be pointing to the lost temple?" Nick asked.

"I think so. At least I'm pretty sure," Sarah replied. "We just need to figure out which one of these stars represents the location of the city."

"I imagine it will be easier said than done. There are so many stars, even in those three constellations. If one of those stars represents the temple location, how do we figure out which one?"

Sarah stared at the notepad. She shifted her gaze to one constellation and then the other. There was something she'd not really paid attention to before, but now it stood out like a blemish. It was a tiny mark in the bottom corner of the diary's final page. She flipped through several of the other pages to make sure she hadn't missed anything else. Seeing nothing of note, she returned to the last page.

"What are you doing? Max asked.

Sarah put her fingertips on the small quadrangle. "Seen this before?"

Nick leaned in. His eyelids were nearly shut, leaving nothing but the narrowest of gaps as he focused on the small image. "No. I didn't notice that before. It's a quadrangle."

"What does that mean?" Max asked.

Sarah took a deep breath. She looked back and forth between the constellations, the notepad, and the quadrangle on the page. Everything was connected. But how? "How did I not see that before?"

"See what before?" Max asked.

"The Diamond in Lyra," Sarah said. "That must be what the quadrangle means."

"For those of us who aren't astronomy geeks," Nick asked, "maybe you could fill us in on exactly what it is you're getting at here?"

"The Summer Triangle isn't a constellation. It's a pattern in the sky that links three primary stars."

She checked the picture of Vega first, then Altair, then Deneb. "My. Oh. My. God," she said.

"Would you please stop doing that and just tell us what's going on?"

Sarah nodded. "Along the Summer Triangle is the Diamond in Lyra and it is composed of three primary stars: Altair, Deneb, and Vega."

"Okay, I'm following you, but how do we know the location of the last star as it relates to a position here on Earth?"

"Simple. Well, sort of simple." Sarah took the map on the table and laid it out flat. She found Tulum and pressed her finger on it. She marked a dot where she'd been holding the place. Then she located the area where they'd discovered Devil's Falls and made a mark with the pencil.

"These are the two we've seen so far. These places contained the clues to the next. To complete the quadrangle, we have to find the third star."

She returned her attention to the map and tilted her head to the side. Then she reached over and grabbed the notepad, ripped the next page out of the binding, and placed it over the map. She picked up the pencil and traced the lines of the triangle onto the paper, putting dots at every corner.

"That's one way of figuring out the correct angles," Max said.

"I didn't bring a protractor or ruler," Sarah smirked.

Max shook his head, grinning. With the drawing complete, Sarah took the paper and placed it over the map. Ever so gently, she poked the tip of the pencil through the paper and pressed it down on Lyra. Then she pushed the paper flush onto the map. She lifted the map to see how it related according to the locations they'd visited and then twisted the paper around until she estimated the dot on the sheet was directly over the dot that represented Devil's Falls. Again she pressed the paper flat against the map. This time, she took the pencil up from its place and gently drove it through the last dot on the surface. She wiggled it around to make a mark on the map and then pulled both pencil and paper away.

Sarah stood up, and looked at her artwork with the others crowding around to get a better view.

Max pointed at the last dot on the map. "That's where we'll find the golden algae."

Nick frowned. "There isn't much out there. Wild jungle, mostly. Although there are a few inhabitants."

"Tribes of people who keep to themselves, wildlife, and ghosts."

The two turned to look at Nick, puzzled.

"Wait a minute, ghosts?"

"Well, they're not literally ghosts. At least I hope not. That's just what some of the locals call them. I've only heard rumors, stories, of men who protect the jungle in that region. Maybe some tribal natives or something like that."

"Lucky, I don't believe in ghosts."

"Yeah, but that doesn't mean you shouldn't be careful. Anyone who has wandered into that area has never come out. Look at all the missing explorers."

***

Luci lay quietly after Calisto administered the draught to her. The liquid slid down her throat and Luci felt no pain, just a soothing warmth. She relaxed as she gazed around a staircase configuration made up of 170 terraces built in a completely different style from the Incas.

Not long ago, on an archeological dig, she visited Ollantaytambo, which had been the royal estate of Emperor Pachacuti. It was at the time of the Spanish conquest of Peru and served as a stronghold for the Inca resistance.

The emperor had built some of the most beautiful and impressive temples in the world. An excellent example of the architecture is Machu Picchu, rediscovered in 1911 by Hawaiian historian Hiram Bringhame after it lay hidden for centuries above the Urubamba Valley. The "Lost City of the Incas" is invisible from below and completely self-contained, surrounded by agricultural terraces and watered by natural springs. Although known locally, it was mostly unknown to the outside world. This city, Luci thought, is probably one of those cities that time had long forgotten. But the people here, Calisto, her daughter…they look Greek. How was that possible?

"Luci," Calisto said.

Startled out of her dreams, Luci looked up at her.

"Your friends are close by. My people have found them."

Elated that they were all alive, Luci gingerly got up. The pain was gone from her leg. "I can't thank you enough, I am so grateful to you, Calisto."

"No one can ever know about this place. It is our own land, with our own laws. We don't want people from outside invading us."

"I promise we won't tell anyone about you or your lands. Is it possible though to have a sample of the mykite that you put on my leg to heal it?"

Calisto walked briskly away.

***

Max woke up to an eerily quiet campsite. He walked over to Sarah and Nick, nudging them. When they looked up, he put his index finger over his lips. Max and the group tiptoed out of the tent and found no one. The Russians who had captured them were gone. It was as if they were ghosts and had just vanished.

They sat together by a fire that was still burning and stared with exhaustion at the flames. "What now?"

The air smelled of death, the acridic smell of blood. But there was no evidence of anyone or anything.

"We have everything we need to find Luci and the lost city. Let's retrieve our gear and get the hell out of here before they come back."

"Something tells me they're not coming back, not ever," Nick said.

"What do you mean?" Sarah asked.

"Look in the bushes. There's a man standing just past the tree line." He pointed.

The man crept forward as if walking on air. He advanced toward Max, pointing a gun in his face. "You will come with me," he said.

Max recognized him as one of the cooks. "I don't think so. Your friends don't play nice."

"You can stay here and get killed like the others."

"As if that explains it all, and all is forgiven," Sarah said with arms crossed.

"I will take you safely to Luci."

"Lead the way," Max said, immediately.

Sarah and Nick looked questioningly at him. He nodded, and they picked up their gear and followed the man.

***

"I thought that man was leading us to the Lost City," Sarah said.

"Possibly, but maybe he's not who we think he is. He was with the Russians even if he was a cook, for God's sakes."

"But if he is from the Lost City, then he knows now that we're not guerrillas or Russians."

"Yeah, I'd say that helped a lot."

"It would've been nice if they had also given us back our ammunition and guns," Max said.

Birds squawked in the canopy. Rainwater from a storm that went through an hour before dripped onto the group intermittently. Most of the forest floor was covered in leaves, twigs, and debris, though the animal path they were on had thick patches of mud that drove the group off course for a few yards at a time.

Max stopped by a huge tree and pulled out his map. They'd been tracking toward the point Sarah had drawn the night before, checking every twenty minutes or so to make sure they were being led the right way. The hike had already consumed two hours, and

Max wondered if they should have brought more water from the river.

"You keep looking at the map. You don't trust our new-found guide?" Sarah asked.

"I think we need to keep our options open just in case," Nick answered.

"According to the map," Max said, "It can't be too far now. Just over that next ridge, and we should be right on top of it."

"I hope you're right." Nick wiped his forehead with his forearm. "I gotta tell you, I cannot wait to get out of this heat."

Max laughed and raised an eyebrow. "This humidity is something else, isn't it?"

"This humidity is bad. Nowhere I've ever been can touch this."

"At least the rain cools us off now and again," Sarah added. "Come on...Let's get going, we have Luci to find."

Max stuffed the map in his backpack and pressed on down the hill, grabbing low-hanging tree branches along the way to keep from slipping and busting his tailbone.

The downhill part wasn't so bad, but the hard work began at the bottom of the ravine, where they started the difficult task of climbing. It took nearly an hour for the four to make it two-thirds of the way to the top, where they stopped again to drink some water and catch their breath.

They didn't talk much while they recovered. The cook stood up and began walking again, Max made a weary motion to the others, and they got going once more.

Arriving at the top of the ridge brought relief to everyone's face. Then they were given a small reward for their efforts: the crest rounded at the top, and the thick group of trees parted slightly to provide a magnificent view of the foothills and jungle spreading out over many miles.

Down the other side of the mountain, a roundish basin lay ahead, almost like a giant bowl had been placed there millennia ago to imprint the land.

Max took a long drink of water and looked over the setting. "The city should be somewhere down there in that basin."

"That's a big area to cover. Hey, are you sure we're going in the right direction?" Nick asked.

The guide nodded.

"The Greeks were extremely precise with their designs and construction. If we've calculated correctly, this is the place. The Lost City should be somewhere in the center." Max pointed.

"If our calculations are right," Sarah said.

Max's eyes caught a movement in the jungle, and he snapped his head to the right. "We're not alone."

***

Unable to run, Luci stared at the two ghosts. Terror prickled her neck. Every hair on her body stood on end, and her pulse accelerated into a frenzy.

The ghosts didn't move. Neither were they floating. They seemed real, with definite shapes.

Weren't ghosts invisible with only an aura of white?

Her breathing calmed. Curiosity getting the better of her. Taking the plunge to discover more, she stepped closer. They didn't move. Another step closer.

Luci couldn't believe her eyes. She was looking at the father and son who had vanished years before in the Amazon. The father had sent a compass back to his wife to prove that he had not died. But that was the end of it, or was it?

What were they doing here? "Your names are Percey and Jack Fawcett. Or am I dreaming all of this?"

"You're not dreaming. We wanted to come and visit Calisto's latest guest."

"Wait a minute, you guys disappeared around 1925. How can you still be alive?"

"We were ambushed by Calisto's people and given a hearing of sorts. They couldn't figure us out. We weren't of their world, nor were we of our own world. We were declared spirits, and figured we belonged somewhere, but where? They brought us here. By the way, what year is it?"

"This is insane. The year is 2020," Luci declared.

"How is my mother?" Jack asked.

"I'm sorry, she must have passed away many years ago. There was a book written about both of you and your adventures. Just to let you know, your wife never stopped believing that you were still alive."

"Did she receive my compass?"

"Yes, Mr. Fawcett, she did, and never gave up hope that you or Jack remained alive."

"That's my girl, she was a trooper."

"I can't believe I'm here speaking with you. How are you still alive?" Luci asked.

"That golden elixir that Calisto gave you to heal your leg. Well, it truly is a miracle drug."

"I believe it could heal so many people in the world."

"Calisto won't let you take any of it out," Jack answered.

"Now, why would that be?" Luci asked, incredulously.

"That is the reason we were never able to leave. It keeps us alive. Muri won't let it go to the outside world. She knows if it gets out, this world will be gone."

"I wouldn't tell anyone where I got it."

"Maybe not you, but someone will find a way to backtrack the way you came in and figure out where you had been. Am I right?"

"Possibly," Luci answered, reluctantly. "Calisto's people are bringing my friends here."

"I think you should all plan to spend a very long time here," Percey Fawcett answered.

***

"I don't see anything, Max," Nick whispered. He had crouched low, watching what was before him.

Less than a minute later, something flew from one tree branch to another about two hundred yards away.

"There," Max said.

"I saw it," Sarah exclaimed. "Maybe a monkey?"

"No, I don't think so," Max quietly replied.

The man with them, their cook and so-called guide, turned around and ran in the opposite direction.

"I guess you were right, maybe our guide wasn't who he said he was."

Max shrugged.

"Why? Do you think it's one of those ghosts we heard about?" Sarah asked.

Max didn't answer, but if he had to guess, that's what he would have thought. "Maybe. I'm pretty sure I saw a human leg, but it was covered in dark gray and green paint. Camouflage?"

"In this area, it would be a great cover."

Something didn't feel right. Max had experienced the same feeling many times before something terrible happened. The birds no longer chirped or sang in the treetops. There were no signs of any wildlife either. No snakes or mammals crawling through the branches or on the ground. The entire forest had gone quiet. More than that, an ominous feeling hung in the air: dread.

"This is creepy," Sarah said, looking around her. "I think it's time to get out of here."

She started to get up, but Max put his hand on her back and kept her down low. "If you go now, they'll see you."

"They already do. This place is cursed. We shouldn't be here," Sarah said.

"There's no such thing as ghosts. You know that," said Max.

"I just saw a leg wrapped around a tree trunk."

Sarah followed Max's finger until she saw the two legs, with feet planted on two opposing limbs. The person's arms also encircled the tree. A weapon hung off his back. She couldn't see the face, only shoulders.

"It's a man, and he's preying on your fears. Don't give him that power. They're just people."

"This doesn't look good. How many are out there?"

"There's no telling how long they've been watching us."

"Does anyone have any ideas on how we're going to get away from here?" Sarah asked.

"I think we can forget that thought completely."

"Why, because it isn't your plan?" Sarah seethed between closed teeth.

"No, because they're looking at us right now."

Everyone followed Nick's gaze up into the trees and realized what had him spooked. Dozens of men with paint covering most of their bodies stood on tree branches. Several had bows and arrows, others had blowguns held to their mouths, aimed at them.

The first man they had seen said, "You need to come with us."

"No," Max said.

"Do you want to see your friend, Luci?" he asked.

"Do you know where Luci is?"

"She is in our city."

"Is she okay, is she hurt?" Sarah asked.

"Calisto has healed her. She is fine now."

"You speak English very well. How did you come about learning to speak it?"

"Two men of the outside world. They taught us."

"Were they English, because you have a bit of an accent."

"I don't know. I've never lived anywhere but here."

Pointing to their guide, Sarah asked, "Is that man dead?"

"No, not yet. He was with a group of men who had taken you prisoner. They are all gone now."

"I think we need to follow them back, and get Luci," Max said. Although he wasn't sure these men wouldn't kill them as well.

The tall man nodded, and the other men lowered their weapons. "You follow us. We will take you back to our home."

***

Their new guide led his own men down the trail, through the last remains of acrid gun smoke and past the ghosts waiting and watching their every move.

Sarah looked around to make sure that everyone was still together. A shallow stream cut through the jungle, winding its way between trees and through a ditch that divided the foot of the ridge from the rest of the basin.

Max kept his eyes peeled as the procession crossed the creek, venturing more in-depth into the forest. They marched for ten minutes before their guide, his hand shooting up, halted the group.

Max motioned for the others to stop. He peered into the jungle through the thick foliage.

"So, where's the temple, and how long does it take before we get there?" Max asked.

"It's not far, according to our new guide. Apparently, these men have been placed here to protect and guard the entrance to the Lost City," Nick said, looking at his map.

"There has to be something important down there if all these guys are willing to die for it," Sarah added. Quietly she said, "Are you sure we can trust these men? Do you think they were sent by Luci, or is there something else going on?"

Max turned his head. He was standing just out in front of the rest of the group, on the other side of a large rock shaped like a dead serpent. His eyes, however, were turned slightly to the right. They followed his gaze to a boulder sticking out of the ground. On the side of the rock, almost invisible to the naked eye, was a figure carved into the stone.

Sarah took a cautious step toward the boulder watching for snakes. She stopped at the base of a rock and bent. She touched the carving with her index finger and ran it along the outline. It was a cross. "We're close," she said.

"Look for two more rocks like this one. They should have another cross and a diamond."

"They trudged through the jungle, the men cutting their way through the overgrowth with machetes in one hand while still holding their weapons steady with the other. All manner of giant leaves, branches, and vines blocked their movement and made progress slow and methodical.

The creek bent to the right and meandered off through the jungle. Max traced the stream across the valley and noticed something jutting out of the bank next to it.

"Over here," Nick said. "Another boulder. Could be a marker."

"Shouldn't they already know where the markers are?" Nick picked up his pace, pushing back the leaves and making his way toward the creek where the second boulder stood out from the dirt.

"We're going a different path, there was a landslide that blocked the entrance we came through. We had to hurry so we could catch up with you before you got into any more trouble," answered the tall man.

Max continued to follow his own clues not trusting that this man was really taking them to Luci. He pointed at the side. "There it is. A diamond."

"Now, we have to find the last marker." Sarah looked down at the map she had made and remembered the Summer Triangle. She turned toward the center of the basin and pointed. "That means the last marker should be somewhere in that direction."

Nick took the lead, walking out in front of the others, cutting his way through leaves and limbs, moving faster now that he sensed how close they were to their goal.

Ten minutes into it, he stopped and wiped his forehead. Sweat poured off everyone in the group. Their damp clothes stuck to their skin, making things even more uncomfortable.

"You okay, Sarah?" Nick chopped down another broadleaf with his machete.

"Yeah, I'm in heaven."

He whipped his blade through the air and sliced across another cluster of huge leaves. Suddenly, the forest opened. Space before them was devoid of most vegetation save for a stand of trees growing sporadically here and there. While it seemed unnatural, the clearing wasn't what struck Max.

It was two stones jutting out of the ground about thirty feet directly in front of them. One was broken at the base and lying on its side; the other still stood upright.

Max stared with wide eyes at the stones. When he spoke, his voice was a whisper, "This is it. This is the gateway to Luci and the lost city, I'm sure of it."

The guide looked on stoically.

***

Katerina took Luci to a room within the temple. It was beautifully decorated. She wondered how they were able to get such finery. A bath had been drawn for her, and she was more than happy to get out of the clothes she had been wearing for the last week. She smelled, her hair was dirty, and she really needed to shave her legs.

She undressed and left her clothes on the floor, wondering what she would do with them—toss them or get them clean and sewn. She soaked and washed, wondering if it was true what the Fawcetts had said: would she be made to stay here?

They must have some conveniences here somewhere around the temple. She walked into a large room right off her bedroom, amazed at the solid gold sunken bathtub. Floral scents and soap lay beside the tub, with a towel and a robe to put on after drying herself.

She stepped into the tub gingerly to see how hot the water was; it was perfect. She plunged in all the way, immersed her hair and just lay there on her back. In so many ways, she didn't want to leave here. The people were warm and friendly. They never became ill, there was beautiful artwork surrounding her, and everywhere she had walked that day, the kids were laughing, playing, and that was at school.

There was a knock at the door.

"Yes, can I help you?"

"Yes, madam, Luci. We are leaving some clean clothes and are taking your clothes to be cleaned and repaired."

"Thank you, but if you just show me where I can do it myself..."

"It is truly not a problem. We are only happy to help our guests to become acclimated to our homeland."

Really? "Again, thank you."

She stepped out of the tub, dried off, and placed the silken robe around her. She walked into the room and saw a magnificent set of silk dresses for her to wear. Right now, she thought, I'm just too tired to think about all of this. She lay on the bed and fell asleep.

Luci woke to the incredible smell of coffee and bright daylight streaming into the room. She climbed out of bed and followed the scent into the plaza outside her doorway. The square, Luci learned, was called Huacapata, the most important religious building. It was magnificent, covered with sheets of gold and silver. Gold was a sacred metal thought to be the sweat of the sun and the tears of the moon. Luci believed that the building had to be serviced by a staff of thousands long ago. High priests and priestesses who served the Gods. These women were chosen for their beauty and worked in a secluded convent called the Acllahuaci. They helped by cooking food for the Gods, weaving beautiful clothes for the Sapa Incans, and making daily offerings to the Gods. The Incans must have lived or co-existed here at one time.

March 1536

Leaping into the air, Calisto tackled the giant Incan warrior leaning over her mother. He fell back, more overcome with surprise than hurt.

The leader dropped the bucket and reached to grab her. Calisto darted under his arms and spun back. She grabbed the bucket, dumping it over his head. Using the point of her reed-woven sandals, she stomped his toe with all her strength.

"Mitera!" she cried out.

Then, with both hands, she barreled toward the unbooted warrior, uttering another scream. Her body smacked against him, shoving him into the fire. His frightened yelp echoed inside the bucket in the fireplace. She spun around, grabbed the hair-matted dagger, and hurled it into the flames.

The Incan dropped her mother and scrambled to his feet, cursing.

Calisto dived to her knees and grabbed two of the quills still drying on the edge of the hearth. With the instinct of a killer, she spun back to face him. And plunged the quills deep into his eyes.

The Incan's screech filled the room. He gripped the quills, trying to pull them out, but tottered around like a drunk. He stumbled into the man on the ground, then banged into the wall and passed out.

Beside the pile of clothing still to be packed away, Calisto spotted her ink-stained chemise. As she bent to grasp it, the barefoot Incan came at her from behind.

His arms snatched at her. She threw the chemise over his head, which caught in the loop of muslin that descended over the two of them. She yanked hard on it, jerking him into her back as the chemise suffocated him. Even though she had no chance against all three, she had to maim at least one. When the others came at her, she'd fight.

The man holding the tongs into her mother let go and jumped up. Calisto bared her teeth at him. He lunged at her with his large leather glove.

Calisto instinctively took a deep breath a second before the glove clamped over her mouth. She struggled against him for a long moment. She had to save her mother.

Nothing else mattered.

Without air to fuel her, Calisto's strength ebbed away. Her grip on the chemise behind slackened and the barefooted Incan's head came free. He grabbed her hands and twisted the chemise around them. In front of her, the leather-clad Incan held the glove over her mouth with his other hand on her throat.

Calisto took one last glimpse of her mother's bloodied breasts and looked into her eyes.

March 18, 2020

Luci got used to the rhythm of life at New Helike.

It became almost routine as she waited for Max, Sarah, and Nick to find her. She used the time to watch children being taught in an open classroom in the center of town. The children were all beautiful, and their parents were kind and giving. This was a place where she would love to live for the rest of her life. Unfortunately, she had responsibilities at home. As time went by, she couldn't remember much of what those responsibilities were, though.

She had her own little villa with bougainvillea running up the walls. She even started her private garden and watered the seeds hoping to see them grow into mature plants: maize, potatoes, grains, legumes. She couldn't wait to share them with the people within the walls of the temple. Several of the children had brought different fruits for her to try. She had been given a goat and a horse as a neighborly gift.

Not far from her villa was a cave with a waterfall and fish for cooking and eating. The fish were in abundance. They practically jumped into her basket.

There were hundreds of manmade terraces built to ensure proper drainage and soil fertility, which also protected the mountain from erosion and landslides. There seemed to be only twelve acres of land which grew corn and potatoes which seemed to be able to support over 750 people, plus the goats, cows, horses, and the fruit that was all over the place.

Walking around the area, Luci could see that the location of the temple had natural defenses with its deep precipices and steep mountains. It sat in a saddle between two peaks with a commanding view down two valleys and a nearly impassable mountain at its back. It had its own natural water supply from springs.

Near the cavern, Luci spied what looked like a secret passageway in a gap in the cliff, but the only way you could get across was by a tree-trunk, and the gorge below was daunting.

How was she ever going to get her and her friends out of here when they finally arrived...if they did?

***

Nick stepped toward the two big rocks, still eyeing them with an intense, analytical stare. Max followed his friend, noting the way the men were staying close, almost like they were there to prevent them from getting away instead of being there for protection. Maybe he was over thinking. Then again, Max knew his instincts. They'd saved his hide more times than he could count. If something didn't feel right, that usually meant it wasn't.

"These stones…" Nick said. "There was a part of the diary that mentioned stones that acted as sort of an external gate to the temple."

"What's this?" Sarah stepped around Max to get a closer look.

"The entrance to our city is close." The tall man pointed at the stone on the left. "There's the second cross."

"So this isn't it, is it?" Sarah sounded disappointed.

"We're close," he replied.

"But if there were anything like that lying around, we'd probably see it by now. It's been several centuries since this place was last documented. I'd say it's likely buried by dirt and other debris."

"It is a camouflage to keep people unaware of our existence."

"So, how do we know what we're looking for?" Max asked.

Nick stood silent for a moment, staring beyond the two stone structures and into the jungle. Not far away was a mound covered in trees, leaves, bushes, and rocks. It looked like any other mound in the middle of a forest. At first glance, no one would think anything of it. Max, however, thought otherwise.

"Don't worry, I think we've found the entrance," he said. The guide nodded in affirmation.

Nick stepped toward the little hill. "That's why it's been so difficult to find. I bet the explorers have walked right by it multiple times and never realized it."

"It's been closed off for a very long time," their guide said.

"Let's look around for something out of place, possibly unusual."

"Like a pile of rocks, maybe a smaller mound of dirt that seems moved. Any kind of thing that looks out of the ordinary."

"We're in a jungle. Everything looks unusual," Sarah said.

"Why are you both questioning everything? Our guide and his men know where they're going."

"Yes, but just in case they're leading us in the wrong direction."

"So little trust, Nick," Max said, smiling.

They moved forward, leaving the gate behind and spread out into three columns along an old path leading toward the mound. Something strange stuck out of the ground ahead. Max and Nick slowed until they were close. Max picked up the object, wary there could be a snake or something else hiding underneath.

"It's Luci's. It's a ring her grandmother gave her," Sarah said.

Sarah moved vines and shrubs away from the rocks, searching frantically for the entrance.

"If this hill is covering the temple, there must be a way in somewhere," Max said.

The group made their way along the path until they were at the base of the hill. They encircled the earthen structure and looked painstakingly around the area for any sign of something that could be an entrance. They kicked rocks, leaves, sticks, and other debris out of the way.

After nearly an hour of intense searching, they found nothing more of Luci's.

Max ran the sleeve of his shirt across his brow to remove the sweat for what had to be the fifth time since they began looking for Luci's belongings.

"This is the spot," Sarah said. She could feel Luci, call it a gut feeling. They were in the right place, and she knew it. That didn't mean it wasn't time to dump the machetes and consider bringing in some equipment to aid in the search.

"You need to come with us into the entrance of the cave. No more looking for trinkets."

A scream ripped through the silence, cutting off whatever Max was about to say.

Max swallowed hard and looked at Nick and Sarah. He had had a bad feeling about this whole situation.

March 1536

Calisto finally came to and found she was gagged with her ink-stained chemise shoved into her mouth. Tied to one of the kitchen chairs, she opened her eyes to see her mother still on the floor.

In her fury, she never gave a thought about her own life, everything she'd done had been in the hope of saving her Mitera.

"She's awake," said a voice near to her ear.

A hot stick from the fire glowed at the front of the hearth.

"Close your eyes, and you'll get the same treatment you gave my friend," the leather-clad Incan said.

Calisto's eyes slid to the left to see him slumped against the wall with her mother's apron wrapped around his head.

Keeping the glowing poker in front of her face, the bare-footed Incan forced her to look at her mother. Once again, the lead warrior lifted the poker out of the flames and clamped it to her mother's breast. Her Mitera screamed and fainted.

Calisto screeched into the gag. She struggled against the ropes, ignoring the string that was rubbing her arms raw. In her attempt to get closer to her mother, she shunted the chair aside. One of its legs rocked on the uneven floor, and the chair crashed. Calisto's head slammed against the stone slabs, sending a jolt of pain through her body.

This position gave her a worse view of her Mitera's injuries.

The leather-clad Incan ripped the poker out of her mother's breasts, the claws shredding her soft skin.

Calisto lay still, her head pounding. The warrior left her mother bleeding while they finished the stew and discussed what to do with her.

The leader poked a boot into Calisto's side. "Where is the golden potion?"

Calisto widened her eyes, and her mouth went dry.

"If you do not give us this mykite to take to our leader, you will face the same fate as your Mitera."

Sudden dizziness filled Calisto's head. *How did they know about the mykite?*

March 18, 2020

"What do you think that was?" Nick asked.

"Someone screamed, but I don't know where from," Max answered.

The group looked around, assessing their surroundings. The walls were cut smooth from the rock in the earth. The hole leading to the surface dropped into a vast dome-shaped room.

"This doesn't look like a temple," Nick said. "Maybe a deathtrap."

"Whoever or whatever created this," Max said, "didn't use primitive tools. They had some kind of technology."

"What do you mean?" Sarah asked.

"You can't get that clean a bore through the rock with a hammer and chisel. I mean, you could, but it would take centuries to get this deep and get it so clean. Not only that, but you'd also have to have an army of skilled craftsmen to do it. This looks like it was done by a machine."

"Unless it did take thousands of years."

"Who'd be alive, unless it was an ongoing project?"

"What are you saying?" Max asked. "That either the people who built this had modern technology or they're thousands of years old?"

Sarah rolled her shoulders. "Wouldn't be the first time we encountered something strange."

"Hey, look over here. See the decorative carvings around the spikes?" Max pointed his flashlight at one of the nearest cones. "That's a Greek hieroglyphic."

Max stood off to the side of the circle of deadly spikes where the floor was tiled with large, smooth stones similar to those he'd seen in so many city streets. He put his beam on the far wall in what he thought was the direction of the mound above. He lowered it until the broad circle of light hit something out of the ordinary at the base where it met the floor.

"What is that?" Nick asked.

His question drew Sarah's attention. She turned her light in the same direction.

"Looks like a pile of rocks." Max moved slowly toward it, minding every step in case there were other traps in place. As he drew near, he could see what happened. "This corridor is blocked."

"It is the way in," their guide said. "The earth must have shaken these boulders loose."

Max, Sarah, and Nick placed their lanterns on the ground around the pile of stones to light the area while others began removing the rocks one by one. Some were heavier and required two pairs of hands to get them out of the way. The three formed a line and passed the rocks from one to another to keep them out of the way.

"Wait, what does that mean?" Nick pointed at a dark engraving over the entryway. The image looked like it was half primate, half-human. The creature was in a seated position with its knees pulled toward its face.

At the temple entrance, Nick, Max, and Sarah removed the last of the rubble.

"That's Yut Cimil," their guide said, pointing to the engraving.

"Who is that?" Sarah questioned.

He laughed when he saw the befuddled look on her face. "The Greek God of Death."

"That isn't all, Yum Cimil was the changer of the earth and sky. The Greeks believed that when the time was right, he would return to earth and cleanse the world of evil and return it to a state of balance," Nick added.

A man Max didn't recognize from before fired his gun at their guide. Max spun to the other men as the guy whipped his weapon out to the fire. Max grabbed the barrel and jerked him forward, smashing his elbow into the man's nose. Blood poured from the broken appendage as the guy clutched at his wound with both hands.

The Greek guide slid down the wall holding his stomach and groaning in agony.

The cook who had offered to take them to find Luci and the temple at the camp took out his gun and aimed it at Max. He swung his gun into the guy's jaw, knocking him out instantly. Nick jammed his muzzle into the man's gut and squeezed the trigger. Bullets tore out of the man's back, flying dangerously toward Sarah.

Sarah dove out of the way, narrowly dodging the deadly barrage.

March 1536

Shouting that he needed the golden elixir to take to his leader, leather-clad man slammed his boot into Calisto's body.

"Where is it?" he screamed, bringing another boot closer to her face.

Calisto jerked her head back, knowing it would only take one hard kick to smash her jaw.

"Answer me, or you'll get the same beating as your Mitera," he said, pointedly looking down at her sick mother.

"She will get more than a beating." The barefoot warrior leered at her. "I want her first."

"No, I will be first, and I will take my time to punish her where it hurts most. She will beg for mercy, but she will tell us all we want to know."

Leatherman shrugged. "I am the senior here, I will have her first."

They banged their fists on the table and began to fight.

Calisto took no notice. She focused her mind on other things, but questions tumbled around. Her arms twitched against the ropes. How could she escape? And how could she get her Mitera to a safe place?

A loud bang on the door jolted her out of her nightmare. A fourth man booted it open and bellowed, "Who is next on the watch?"

Leatherman bellowed at the younger man, "You are. Get back to your post."

"There are other men here who want the women. They also believe they are women vampires, and they're to be burned."

March 18, 2020

"What the fuck. You lost them, you moron?" shouted Ivan slamming his fist on the cherry wood desk.

"Everyone is dead. Xander, the men hired for the expedition, Alexy, and now the cook. I had to stay back because Sarah knows me," Sergei screamed at his boss.

"Why didn't you stop them before they crossed through the volcano?"

"We tried. We were working with the Peruvian cartel. Xander was shot. He texted and tried to tell me where Max and crew were headed, but he died before he finished."

Sergei's answer didn't please Ivan, but it gave him a clue what he was up against. Night had fallen over the Greek island, and the sounds of the evening carried through the open windows: various insects, birds, and the constant crashing of the sea in the distance. Luci had escaped through his fingers again. "I can have mercenaries sent to you by tomorrow."

"I think we're up against more than Max and his group."

Ivan processed the additional information for a moment. He paced from one end of his home in the compound to the other, stopping before the hut that had housed Sarah. He spun around and stared across the room, looking out at the wooded hills. "From what you've described, it sounds like they have most certainly found clues to the Lost City in the jungle. I can't believe Xander didn't grab the diary or map, or both, away from them."

There was a tense moment of quiet between the two men. Finally, Sergei broke the silence. "I saw painted men watching our targets, and before those men took them out of the encampment, Xander placed a homing device in Luci's notebook and remember Sarah still has one in her arm."

"So they're close. Give me your GPS coordinates, I'll have the men helio into where you are. Then get going."

"What do we do with Sarah when we catch up?"

Ivan laughed subtly. Sergei had developed a less than gentle touch over the years. He seemed even more vigorous when it came to his lustful side. Ivan knew what kinds of twisted things Sergei was capable of. His reputation for cruelty was something Ivan had needed to ensure things always went his way. He was also the only person on the planet whom Ivan felt he could trust. Sergei had gotten rich off of him, but he rarely forgot his place. It could be deadly.

"I may just let you have your fun with her, my old friend."

***

"I think we're on our own, Max."

"I guess we get out of the cave and follow the stars. That was what we figured out," Max said.

"There have been so many signs already. I know we're close," Sarah said. Taking the diary, she reexamined the lines. Her finger traced the passages a couple of times before she looked up from the page. "We head west."

Deep forest awaited just beyond the rock. At the edge of the woods, twisted ancient trees stood hauntingly silent in the faint light of night like something out of a horror film. As they walked deeper into the forest, Sarah's ears filled with the sounds of the woods, and, as when she arrived, her nose enjoyed the sweet smells of nature. In the clearing where the house was situated, the cloudless sky that opened up above was absolutely breathtaking. With no moon visible, the number of stars dotting the canvas of night seemed infinite.

What would the entrance to the Seven Golden Caves look like? The events of the past two weeks were unfathomable. She felt a calm come over her, a feeling of detachment and contentment.

A shooting star burst through the black sky, shaking her from her thoughts, It only lasted a couple of seconds before burning out.

Max and Nick woke her out of her reverie. "What are you stopping for?"

"No reason, just watching the shooting star," Sarah said, pointing skyward.

"Did you make a wish?" Nick asked playfully.

"Of course, it'd be silly not to." She grinned.

"Okay, I give, what did you wish for? I hope it's to find the city, find Luci, and get home."

"No, it wasn't that, but I can't tell you what I wished for, then it might not come true."

The group stood in a clearing in the forest, staring up into the universe. Constellations and random clusters of stars blended together in the elaborate cosmic tapestry.

"Yeah, you can sure see a lot of shooting stars out there. No city lights to intrude on anything.

"That's it!" Max exclaimed.

"What?" The other two were startled by the sudden excitement and spoke in unison.

"The falling stars!" Max said. "Name the stars. You get it?" Max went on, "Meteors, or shooting stars, as we call them, were sometimes called the chariots of the gods in ancient times. The chariot was a common conveyance, so whoever created the myths simply applied it to the story as a necessary detail for the ordinary human."

"I get it, sort of. You mean like those pictures of a Greek God riding a chariot?"

"So what does ancient mythology have to do with the Seven Golden Caves in South America?" Sarah placed her hands on her hips.

"Sarah, look at your computer. See if there was a significant meteoric event ever recorded anywhere in South America. I'm talking cave drawings, stone carvings, anything you can see."

"You mean like we saw in the cave, those drawings we did of them?"

They huddled around Sarah's computer and saw several drawings similar to what they had seen in the caves. "I think I know where the next clue is. See that rock formation on the screen? Now look ahead, doesn't the shape remind you of a chariot?"

Nick shook his head while Sarah responded with a slight nod. "Yes, I think so."

The group hurried to the large boulders just past the caves ahead. They reached them and noticed the strange markings. It's ancient Greek, similar to what Luci translated before she went missing."

"There has never been a single document that I know of that match those carvings or closely resemble what is on those stones." He held up his hand, pausing in mid-thought. "And that is exactly what the riddles have been leading us to look for—these ancient stones." It marks the path of those who are seeking the seven caves, but also the way of the Chariots of Heaven.

"How are we going to decipher the writings without Luci? I certainly failed."

"I haven't quite figured that out, but I do know we have a big day ahead of us. It's too dark to walk any further, so let's set camp, and get some sleep."

"Good night, then." Sarah popped open her tent, threw her sleeping bag inside, and zipped the canopy shut.

March 1536

Calisto gasped at the young warrior's declaration of a vampire about to be burnt nearby. Like her, the unbooted Incan seemed to be in a stupor about the news.

"Tlahuelpuchi!" The unbooted warrior frowned. "Heretics are supposed to be punished by our people."

Leather-clad Incan snorted. "Some of us get bored with insignificant punishments. They should all burn."

"Come on. Let's go watch."

Still slumped over in his chair, the unbooted Incan protested, "We can't leave. We are on duty. Besides, I can't see anything." He stood.

The young warrior at the door hesitated, looking from one man to the other at the table. "They said it is only a few hours from here."

The leather-clad Incan rose to his feet and strode to the door while the unbooted warrior yanked on his sandals and glanced at Calisto. "What about them?"

Shutting her eyes with her chin looking on her chest, Calisto pretended to be asleep.

"Leave them here. We'll come back to give the young one something she won't forget."

"She's crazy; she'll break free." The now-handled warrior threw on his pack from the back of the room.

"How she's tied up and gagged, she has nowhere to go." The young Incan frowned.

"She's deadly. I don't trust her," the now-sandaled Incan said. "We know what she's capable of."

"Okay, let's go, but we better make it fast."

Calisto listened, hoping and praying the temptation to watch women slowly die at the stake would take them away. Her Mitera lay on her side. Dying.

March 18, 2020

Usually, Luci didn't sleep well other than in her own bed. In fact, traveling in airplanes, buses, and even the occasional metro made it difficult for her to get any kind of rest. For the last hour, however, she'd slept like a log inside her villa.

"Wake up. Your friends are almost here," the accented voice startled Luci wide awake.

During her brief nap, she'd hoped this had all been a nightmare and that she was back home, not worried that none of them would ever be allowed to leave.

"Okay, let me go wash up a bit. Is there any coffee here? I sure could use a cup about now."

"Yes, I'll fetch you a pot of coffee. Do you want cream?"

"Yes, thank you," Luci said with an upward nod.

The sun was bright, coming up over the mountains in the early morning sky. Luci opened her bedroom door and stepped into a vastly different world than she'd left behind in Monterey. All around, the hills of the mountain range were patched with vibrant colors. A light breeze brushed over her, making the air more refreshing than usual. The elevation also dropped the temperature several degrees. Luci was glad she had put on a shawl before stepping out.

A single cloud wisped through the sky high above them as she walked down the garden pathway amongst the grass toward the cave she had been carried through. The view from the top of the mountain was absolutely breathtaking. Why not stay here, she thought. It was more peaceful than she'd ever known.

She stepped inside the cave, she traced symbols, ancient petroglyphs that were probably Greek or Phoenician, with her hand.

"Why have you come here?"

"What?" She turned to see Katerina standing nearby. "You startled me, Katerina. I needed a walk. I remembered that when we originally entered the cave, I noticed the petroglyphs on the walls. I was interested to see if I could decipher them."

"Would you like to see my special cave with a pond that I like to swim in?"

"Yes, but why is it special to you?"

"There are healing mykites there. They helped you. I was going there to pick more when I saw you the other week. I thought you were trying to leave. It is forbidden."

"I would be happy to go with you to your extraordinary place, but I don't understand why leaving here is forbidden. Do you know why?"

"Things are different out there beyond the cave. There have been people who have left, though."

"Do you know what happened to them?"

"I never saw them again. One was a friend I went to school with. Her parents took her away."

"Have you never been curious about the outside world?"

"Percy told me all about it, how cruel people can be, people starving, sickness, and people killing people. I don't think I want to live in a place like that."

"Yes, there are bad things that happen, but there are good things too."

"Can you give me an example of something there that I don't have here?"

"Mmm, let me think for a moment. Have you ever been on a carousel, or had an ice cream cone?"

"No, what are they?"

"Well a carousel goes around in circles, you get to ride on a wooden horse that moves up and down, and the most magical music plays as you go around."

"But my horse does that, and I can play music with it. What's ice cream cones?"

"Well, it's a creamy dessert that is in a type of wafer. On a hot day, you can scoop up whatever kind of flavor you would like and put it in a cone. It tastes sweet, and when you bite into the cone, the flavors explode in your mouth with a crunch."

"Can you make some for me?"

"Do you have any cows?"

"Of course, we do."

"Then, I can make you some."

"What about the cone?"

"I think I might be able to make a wafer to put the ice cream in."

"Since you can make all of this, why do we need to leave?"

"Good question." I wish I had thought about this before answering this knowledgeable young lady. I wonder if she set me up?

March 1536

As the sound of men clattered off into the far distance, Calisto shifted her weight back and forth, rocking the chair closer to the fire. Dawn peeped into the cottage window giving her new hope.

Thankfully, the Incas' brutal lust for bloodshed had given her time to figure out how to escape. Against the hearth, she felt the rough stone's edge on her wrist. Calisto rubbed her arms, sawing at the ropes, her mind focused on getting out before the soldiers came back.

"Mitera? Mitera, can you hear me?"

Her mother lay still.

"Oh, God, please let her be alive."

Calisto couldn't move far with the chair stuck to her back, so she sawed vigorously against the stone ledge.

"Please, please, God, don't let it take ages to cut through a few layers of rope." Her eyes searched the room. Even if she could find something to sever the ropes, she might not be able to right the chair and hobble across the room before the young warrior got back.

"Mitera, Mitera, can you hear me?"

The faintest cry came from her Mitera as she half-opened her eyes and glanced around.

"We are safe, Mitera; they have gone. They will be back, so I need to get these ropes off."

"Calisto." Her Mitera's voice was a hoarse whisper, "When will they be back?"

"A day. Maybe two."

"Get your mykite, Calisto. Hide them in the grotto. They will tear our home and find our secrets. We must keep them safe. Then, you must escape."

"I will take you to the Seven Golden Caves, Mitera. We will hide there until they are gone, or we can find someone to help us."

Mitera lay still and quiet.

"Mitera? Are you okay?" Had her Mitera died?

Calisto glanced around the room one more time. Suddenly a noise outside startled her.

The young warrior stepped through the kitchen door. They were back. Although the thought of someone being burned horrified her, she had hoped they would leave. Maybe the others had left the youngest one to guard her and Mitera.

Now they would never escape.

March 19, 2020

The group departed the valley. The ruins lay undisturbed. They came out of the forest and made their way up the mountain, enveloped in dense fog but just ahead lay an excellent trail that had been cleared giving no possibility of getting lost. The day was wondrous, and the sky full of drifting cumulus.

They crossed the river via a single-log bridge and continued on the trail. They came to a steep slope just below a town with a temple or pyramid in the middle. A group of men stood waiting for them.

"Where is our friend and the men we sent to bring you here?" a large man said.

"They were killed by men who were following us," Max answered.

The village men spoke to one another excitedly and were nervous. In the background, Max heard howler monkeys, which added to the stress they were all feeling.

The mist broke around mid-morning, and a brief rain fell in the weak sunlight. That was when Max spotted Luci coming out of the temple dressed in a Grecian blue gown.

"Geez, what century are you from?" Max took Luci in his arms and squeezing her tight. "We were so worried about you."

"As I was for all of you." Luci gazed over at Sarah and Nick. "I had truly hoped you had left back to Cuzco."

"We would never abandon you. Why would you say that? I'm so happy we finally found you," Sarah said.

"We won't be allowed to leave here."

"That's pure nonsense. Of course, we're leaving and taking you with us," Nick exclaimed.

As the group discussed the problems of leaving, Calisto quietly walked amongst them.

They stopped talking immediately.

"We are a confident, accomplished, and formidable group of survivors," she said. "The people in the outside world have ways that could hurt us and destroy our way of life."

"No civilization has survived forever. Just look at the Romans," Max said.

"I have, but as others face dissolution, like the waves of the sea falling upon the shore, our world is safe here," Calisto said, gesturing with her hands.

This was the first time Luci had seen Calisto's hands up close. They were scared all the way up to her elbow as if she had been in a fire. "You will not bring your ways of living in our homeland. You will adopt our ways, and find happiness and peace, and live a long and fruitful life."

"But, our lives are out there." Max gestured in the direction they had just come.

"You will adjust."

"And if we don't?" Nick asked.

"You will," Calisto said with confidence and walked away.

The villagers from the temple surrounded Max, Luci, and the rest, and they moved back toward the building.

"Fill us in, Luci. Why won't the old lady let us leave?"

"She doesn't want outsiders coming back. The people who were following you are all dead. She will have us killed if we don't stay here and adjust to their way of life."

Max wasn't buying it, or Luci's attitude; she was a fighter. So something was going on. He'd just have to be patient to find out. He walked toward the temple wondering what was going to happen next.

He wouldn't have long to wait.

March 1536

Slumped in her chair, Calisto watched the young warrior digging into the pans on the table. He muttered and went to the pot beside the fire.

"They ate it all!" he cried, scraping out the last bits of meat.

Near the fireplace lay a few scraps of bread. Calisto watched the Incan dunk and stuff a crust into his mouth. Then another. When the bread was gone, he searched the kitchen for more food. The young Incan dipped in and out of clay pots and tossed ladles aside. With a mighty roar, he shoved the remnant of the warriors' meal off the table. The dishes clattered to the floor.

Mitera opened her eyes. "Calisto? Are you ready to go?"

"Mitera, shhh," Calisto whispered, knowing her mother hadn't seen the soldier.

Mitera glanced at the young man and then fixed her eyes on Calisto.

Calisto's heart ached at the look in her Mitera's eyes. Sadness and anguish creased her mother's face as she too accepted their fate. They would die here together.

Unable to find food or water, the young warrior paced the room like a cat ready to pounce. Within minutes, he started coughing, Calisto guessed a crumb of the dried bread had got caught in his throat. He ran to Calisto, leaned over, and grabbed locks of her hair.

"Where is your water?"

"In the well. There is none left here. The warriors drank it all."

"Where is the well?"

"Let me loose, and I will take you there."

Choking out his words, he said, "Do you think me stupid? Do you think I'm a fool? I saw what you did to Anku's eye."

Calisto stared at him, her mind racing. This was her last chance to escape. "It is far down the pathway from our home; you will never find it alone."

His hand shot out and slapped her across the cheek. Calisto fell back. The sharp slap brought tears to her eyes.

"Tell me." The Incan coughed, spitting wet bumps of bread into her face.

"Go down the trail. At the bottom, turn towards the woods. You will see the well hidden amongst the trees."

"If you're lying, I'll cut you."

Without another word, the young Incan walked out the door, running in the direction of the well.

Calisto's heart beat faster. She had sent him in the wrong direction. And had not told him about the barrel beside the house.

She had only minutes to get the ropes off and take her Mitera away from here. Her chin trembled as her gut filled with despair. She would have to burn the cords off her wrists. Even as the thought crossed her mind, Calisto knew the fire's heat would scar and cripple her hands. But she had to think of her Mitera and get her to safety. Her sacrifice to her Mitera would be her hands.

Calisto used her last remaining strength to lumber the chair closer to the fire. Its heat warmed her back. A flame touched her skin.

The ropes had to burn off fast, so she stretched her arms backward, further into the fireplace. White-hot flames licked her hands.

Calisto choked back the scream of pain.

March 22, 2020

Calisto seemed to have aged since she first saw her, Luci thought as she walked down the pathway toward her. Her hair was snow-white, and her light blue eyes indented with lines that seemed more pronounced than before. She was staring thoughtfully, almost dreamily, into the waters of the fountain in the temple.

She looked up and smiled. "I've been waiting for all of you." She studied their faces and nodded. "Yes, you are the ones I've been waiting for. Please, sit down."

"We're not children, Calisto," Max said.

"You are to me. I've lived a very long time. Not that age matters. The soul is eternal." Her smiled faded. "But if the soul is weighed down, it can't see eternity. You understand that, don't you?"

"Yes, I understand that," Luci answered for all of them.

"I thought so. An emissary would sense many things."

"Emissary?" Luci shook her head. "I'm not an emissary. We've come here to ask questions about the mykite."

"I know." She gazed at the roses in the vases standing beside her. "And I will answer."

"Calisto, do you know there are millions of children in this world who have little to eat, and some are so sick they live in hospitals? How sad is that?"

"I wish to ask you how the mykite heals people," Max asked.

"I think you might want to know that a Russian man named Sergei is here asking the same thing."

"So, you are going to give the mykite to the Russians?"

"No, they would not share it with all the people. They cannot be allowed to have that kind of power. They would become Satan on earth."

"They'll be here soon. They're coming very close to hurting so many people, we need to prepare to defend this place," Max said.

"Evil," Luci said.

"You do understand. I thought you might." Calisto nodded. "I've given up everything to be here in New Helike, to save this plant and my people who escaped the volcanoes and the Incans. I did it for mankind."

"No, not mankind. You've not shared it with anyone besides your own people."

"True, but why should I? Nothing really has changed in humans. If the Russians get mykite, they will keep the nations under their thumb. People will die, or they will release a contagion and have the only means to cure it. I failed with my mother. Many years ago, the Incans came to our village to rout out vampires. They almost got the mykite. My mother died for it. I've given up my life to save my people."

"You could save so many more. Children are starving, children who have been abused, neglected, diseased. You could save these children with your mykite."

"I've guarded the golden elixir for all of these years to keep the treasure from being used by those who want only to corrupt. The way to win a war is to leave it alone. I had to protect the mushroom, protect my people. But now I can reach out through you and give back to the world. You can never return here. You will have to cultivate and grow the plants we give you. You will need to care for it, guard it for the children."

"The mykite belongs to all people, not just you," Max said.

"I understand and accept that. You're good people, I've seen that."

"What are you going to do with Sergei?" Sarah asked.

"He will live here for the rest of his life," Calisto said.

"Others will come to find him, to hurt you and your people. Things will never be the same," Max warned.

She leaned back on the bench. "I want to sit here in the sun. Later I will pray and let our Gods decide what is best." She smiled. "I believe they are already at work. After all, they sent me an emissary."

Luci shook her head.

"Don't be afraid. Emissaries don't always recognize their mission." She searched her face. "I think you were sent to do...something. I sense pain within you. Have I hurt you, Luci?"

"No, Calisto, you haven't hurt me."

"Then, I pray your pain will leave you." She looked knowingly at Max. "We won't talk about it anymore. I want you to know you've brought me comfort."

"I don't know why. We can't keep this magical healing fungi a secret. People will want to know where we got it."

"You'll do what you must. But will you stay with us for a little while longer? It's not every day an emissary comes to visit. There's a blessed peace about you." Calisto held out her hands to hold Luci's.

Luci felt a sudden rush of sympathy. Calisto had been wrong, but her motives had been right. She wanted to save her home, the city she had created, her children, and be willing to sacrifice herself to do it. How many other people could say as much? "We will stay a while longer." Luci leaned back and laid her head against the cushions.

"As long as you like, Calisto," Max put his arms around Luci.

***

"Everything okay?" Ivan asked when Sergei answered his SAT phone.

"Xander is dead," Sergei said. "The last message was that he breached the caves and was on the heels of finding the group, the gold, and a healing substance."

"That's not good. You need to find Xander's body. Did he leave his coordinates for you to track him?"

"Yes, I have the mercenaries ready. We were just waiting for a signal from you."

"We're going to make a lot of money for ourselves. I've already retrieved the toxin that we will put in the crops. That little golden mushroom is going to be worth billions. All governments will come crawling to us for a cure."

"What about the gold?"

"That's the icing on the cake."

"I'll see it safely into your hands, sir."

***

Sarah got up from her chair and strolled over to the Greek doors through which Luci and Max had disappeared. She shook her head in wonder as Calisto, Max, and Luci sat together on a bench by the fountain. The old woman had her eyes closed and looked as if she had drifted off to sleep. Luci held her hand and was sitting in silence next to Max.

Sarah couldn't have imagined a more comfortable or tranquil scene. Luci might have been the old lady's granddaughter, and certainly wasn't interrogating her with any degree of urgency. In fact, Sarah could almost feel the bond that drew the old lady and the young woman together. Strange, but no stranger than finding this place.

Her SAT phone rang, and she wondered who could be calling. No one knew—

"Hello, Sarah, beautiful day, isn't it?"

She felt as if she had been kicked in the stomach. "Sergei."

"You're always surprised when I call you. I don't know why. You should know I want to keep in touch. I've made sure that I know where you are, where you go. It seems a long time since our little chat in Greece."

"I was hoping you'd died."

"Yes, it was close. I was very angry with you for escaping. But I wasn't hurt too bad. You only nicked my spleen, and now I'm back."

"That's unfortunate. I'll try to do better next time."

"I'm sure you will. I gained a new respect for you, Sarah. At first, I only wanted to kill you at the earliest possible opportunity. Still, then I realized that nothing has really changed. In fact, my admiration will be like a savory flavor added to our shared experience."

"Why? Why are you doing this?"

"Can you guess? You're such a smart woman."

"Tell me."

"You have to clear the way if you're going to become a god. Witnesses are awkward. No one should be left alive to tell the tale."

"A god?"

"That much money can make a man into a god. That's why I've kept following you. I knew you and Luci would lead me to the fungi."

"You're a monster."

"No one gets in my way. I'm much smarter. I can do what others have not."

She moistened her lips. "And what are you going to do?"

"You and your friends…" He paused. "I have a special plan for Max and Nick. I've decided I'm going to take a long, long time killing them."

Shock and panic rippled through her.

"You're not speaking. Does the thought upset you? I believe I'll let you and Luci watch."

"No. Not Nick and Max." *Don't let Sergei know what his words did to me.* She kept her voice steady. "Who else?"

"So that you can run to the rescue?" His tone turned malicious. "No, you won't ruin my destiny this time."

"Shut up. Don't talk anymore."

"Oh, I did hurt you, didn't I? If I'd had more time, I would have—"

"I said, shut up."

"You can't stop me. Not with Luci. Not with Max. Not with Nick. That's the way to hurt you, Sarah. I remember you were so terribly upset that you couldn't save Max's friend."

"I didn't know that man was Max's friend. Who else is on your list?"

"I think you could guess. But you should really worry about yourself. That's what I want you to do. I want you to sweat. I want you to panic. I want your heart to pound when you hear my voice. Terror is a bit like sex if it's done right. Same moist hands, same tightening of the muscles. Is your heart pounding now, Sarah?"

"No."

"It will. I've neglected you for far too long. Max was too savvy. I had to work around him and do damage control with my boss. But don't worry; I can give you my full attention now."

"By all means. Stop hiding and come out in the open. Maybe you're afraid that I'll manage to kill you. I'm really a very good shot. You would have been dead if you hadn't moved at the last second. Let's see if you can do anything but make threatening phone calls."

He chuckled. "You're taunting me. How very brave...and stupid. It's a beautiful day, and the rose garden is particularly lovely, isn't it?"

Sarah forgot to breathe. She couldn't speak.

"And I believe that our Calisto is taking a little snooze. Your friend Luci must not be a good conversationalist."

"Where are you?"

"At a point where I can see everything you can see. I was disappointed when you didn't follow Max and Luci out to be with Calisto. But I realized it was all for the better. I want you to be last."

"Where are you?" she repeated hoarsely.

"Close enough. My men have you surrounded. I'm also an excellent shot. I'm sighting now..."

"No!" Sarah threw down the phone as she tore through the door. "Get down! She sprinted down the path. "Get down!" she screamed again.

She could see Luci's startled face. Calisto was opening her eyes, straightening on the bench.

"It's Sergei. Get down. He's going to—"

Luci threw herself on Calisto and pulled her to the ground.

A low pop came from somewhere above and behind Sarah. *Luci!*

Luci and Calisto were crumpled on the ground. But there was blood...so much blood.

"No shot!" Sarah said. "I have no shot."

She had to help Luci and Calisto. Sergei must still be up there with his rifle.

Sarah dove sideways. "Luci! Max!" Get down. Sergei—"

"I know." Max was beside her. "Are you okay?"

She nodded jerkily as she tried to pull him to the ground. They rolled behind a large vase full of roses.

"Are you sure it's Sergei?" Max asked. "We caught sight of a shooter on the rooftop next-door when we ran into the garden, but we couldn't identify him. Nick is chasing him."

"I'm sure. Sergei called. He wanted me to know..." She got to her feet. "He wanted me to know he was going to kill Luci, and, oh, my God...everyone."

"Luci?"

Sarah wasn't listening. She was running toward the two people lying by the bench. "She was hit. There was blood..."

"Not my blood." Luci slowly sat up, her gaze fixed on Calisto's face. "I pulled her down, I..."

Sarah stared down at Calisto. A gaping hole had blossomed in the exact center of her forehead. "Very precise. He said he was a good shot," she said dully. "We've got to get out of here. There are other Russians," Sarah said.

"She said I was an emissary," Lucy said. "I don't believe she expected—" She broke off, then said wearily, "Or maybe she did. I don't know..."

"I know we have to get out of here," Max said. "We'll go out the garden gate and—"

"My God." A heavyset, black-haired man with brown skin, in his late forties, stood in the doorway. "What's going on?"

Max stiffened warily. His hand moved to his jacket pockets. "You're our guide to the city."

"Wait," Luci said. "This is one of Calisto's guards. She saved him when he was a boy." She turned to him. "We have to protect New Helike and the people. Where's Katerina?"

There were tears in his eyes, Luci noticed. For a moment, she felt sympathy, then pushed away. "Get the other guards. There are armed men trying to find the mykite. They can't have it. Calisto said I was the emissary. We need your weapons, and we have to leave."

Sarah remembered something else. "Sergei knew where we were. He told me so. It's not logical that he would have been waiting for us here. Could he have bugged me, planted something under my skin when I was out?"

"It's possible," Max said grimly. "No, it's damn probable."

March 22, 2020

Nick hurried down the path; his hair was mussed, and his breath was coming in short pants. "I didn't get him. I think he's headed back to the Seven Golden Caves, Sarah." He looked around. "Where's Max and Luci?"

"There in the garden with Calisto," Sarah said. "Calisto is dead."

"Shit." Nick headed for the temple. "They may need help." He headed toward the garden.

"We'll go together, Nick. We all need to stick together, find the Helikes, and save them from the Russians. They'll never give up the location of the caves. Do you know where Katerina is?" Sarah asked.

"Maybe Luci knows. Sergei may be on the run, but I bet he's gathering reinforcements," Nick said, worriedly.

"You're right. I don't think he's had time to get them here yet. It's only a matter of time. I'm sure Ivan will be with them. That is why Sergei did the killing himself." She shuddered. "Though I'm sure he enjoyed it. You should have heard him on the phone. He was—" She stopped and steadied her voice. "Actually, I'm not his target right now. He wants me to be last. He made me think it was you, Max, or Luci he was going to shoot. He has a list."

"And who is on it?"

"All of us and anyone who gets in his way. He admires himself very much. He says he is very efficient. Kill everyone and leave no witnesses."

"That includes anyone who has defected."

"Yes."

Where were Max and Luci? Sarah was still caught up in the panic caused by Sergei's words. Perhaps she should track down Sergei—

She breathed a sigh of relief, seeing Max and Luci coming out of the temple, followed by two of the Helike guards.

"Calisto said there is a way of closing up the caves so that no one can enter or ever leave again," Luci said. "Let's go to the caves. Calisto was willing to share some of the mykite with us to help all of mankind. She was afraid, and rightly so that the Russians would take it and use it for their own means."

"The guards here are going to help us locate the villagers and get them safely out of the way. Then they'll come with us, and we'll pick up the mykite and leave, hopefully before the Russians come back," Max said.

"Now tell me, Sarah, exactly what Sergei said to you. Every word."

She wouldn't tell them every word. She wouldn't tell him the part that had frightened her almost more than the threat to Luci. The terror hung over her like a dark cloud.

"I'll make it worse for Luci than it was for Gregorio."

March 28, 2020

After relocating the Helike people in the forest far away from the Seven Caves of Gold, Luci went in search of Katerina and couldn't find her anywhere.

"I bet she's already in the caves protecting her people just like Calisto, and her ancestors have done," Sarah said.

"We need to find her before Sergei does and before anyone else gets through those caves.

"How can we trap Ivan?" Sarah asked. "He's like a ghost."

"We start with his phone call to you."

She took a step back. "What do you mean?"

"We have Nick dig out Sergei's number from my cell. When we're all in place, you call him back, and we put a trace on his location. Then we move in for the kill."

"What do you mean 'we'?"

"It has to be in a place we can get to him," Max added. "And so he can't get away like he did in Santorini."

"Won't that be difficult?"

"Yes. Nick is setting up the satellite right now."

"We might not have much time," Sarah said.

"Let's get going then," Luci said.

Max nodded. "Good. We should grab a quick nap and take turns as lookouts. I'll start the first shift."

"Do you want me to stay with you, Max?" Luci asked. She wanted him close enough to touch, close enough to protect.

"Yes, stay with me."

March 1536

Calisto choked on the smell of burning flesh. A sour odor filled her nostrils. She had only ever smelt that dreadful odor once before when her Mitera had roasted a pig and had to rush off to deliver a baby. Calisto had been a child at the time and didn't know how to cook, so she'd ended up burning the family dinner. The sickening stench of her own burning flesh reminded her of the smell when her Patera tanned leather over a flame.

Thinking she was in the middle of a terrible nightmare, Calisto squeezed her eyes tight. When she opened them again, the horror remained; her hands and feet were tied to the chair with Mitera beaten, bruised, and bleeding.

Her Mitera clawed her way to her. "Calisto, Calisto!"

Her mother's voice broke through the haze of pain. Calisto shook her head and tried to focus. The warrior's threat came back. Calisto clenched her jaw against the searing pain in her arms. The young man would not be gone long, and she didn't stand a chance fighting all four of them. Beside her, Mitera tore at the knotted rope. Straining to glance over her shoulder, Calisto once again choked on the stink.

The ropes were burnt and tattered. Long streaks of raw flesh swelled and bubbled up her arms. Under the blackened ropes, her wrists were raw flesh dilated and raw with blisters. Her hands had swollen to double their size. It was the worst pain.

With precise fingers, Mitera picked at the ropes as though plucking the last few beautiful feathers from a slaughtered chicken.

"What are you doing, Mitera?"

"The rope is nearly off, Calisto. Then you must...go." Her mother's voice lifted and dropped in a breathless attempt to save her daughter. "Go to the caves where they will be safe. Run as far and as fast as you can. These Incans will do horrible things to you."

"I can't leave you, Mitera. You must go with me."

"I am not able to walk, Calisto."

"I will help."

"I beg of you!" Mitera's gaze pointed to the back of her legs. "Look."

Only now did Calisto see several deep gashes in her mother's calves. The soldier's knife had done this.

"They severed my muscles, so I cannot walk again."

March 28, 2020

Nick came to Sarah's door just before seven-thirty that evening. "Here it is." He handed her a piece of paper. "I've got to get back to my post. I told Max I needed to take a walk. I'll keep him away until I hear from you or Luci, so he doesn't try to stop you. I don't like this plan of yours at all, but I have to trust your judgment. Just be careful."

Sarah looked down at the numbers on the paper and slowly closed the door. She felt cold with dread and changed her mind. Sarah didn't have to contact Sergei right now. She could go on with Max's plan.

No, she couldn't. She couldn't risk Max ever again. Sarah knew what it would do to Luci.

Sarah sat down and reached for her phone. Okay, get it clear before she talked to him. How was she going to handle him? The principal goal was to set it up for tonight, and in her choice of locations.

What was she thinking? She could be putting Luci in danger. There was no way she could plan everything. Just hearing Sergei's voice made her tremble. Her hand was shaking, so steadied it before she called.

It rang three times.

"Sarah?" Sergei sounded startled.

"Yes, Sergei."

"What an unexpected pleasure. You must have enlisted exceptional help to have located my number. Of course, I was tempted not to answer, but I couldn't resist. However, I'm going to call you back so that you can't trace me. I'll feel safer on my own line." The call disconnected. He called back immediately, but it wasn't Sergei on the line. "Now we can talk. What little scheme have you concocted to try to bust me? Is Max there at your elbow? Let him know I'm going to kill him slowly for ruining everything. Just like he did before at Montsegur to my boss."

"No," she said. "I'm alone."

He was silent a moment. "I believe you're telling the truth. I know you'd lie to me if you could, but I'd know. I learned too much about you during our days together. I studied every tone of your voice, your every movement."

"Because you wanted to know where that damn shard was so you could find the Seven Golden Caves."

"Yes, there is that. It was necessary. But it became so much more, an intense kind of pleasure. You felt it."

"You're demented."

"That has been said by so many people. But those who have said that are not alive anymore."

"What do you want?"

"I want you, Sarah."

"Then I'll come to you."

"A trap, of course."

"No, but I've come to the conclusion that this can't go on any longer. I can't keep looking over my shoulder. You're like a bad dream, and I have to get rid of you and Sergei. I'll choose an open place where you'll feel safe."

"No, I'll choose...if I decide I'm going to let you lure me into your arms. The idea is...compelling."

"I don't care where it is, but I want it to be out in the open, a place for me to run, not be caught like a mouse in a trap. I want my chance at you."

"Now look who's being demanding."

"You said you wanted me to be last. Well, that's too bad. You work on everyone else on your list after me. You kept me in that room and nearly drove me crazy. Everything else came afterward. One way or the other, I'm coming after you tonight."

"Tonight, so eager, Sarah. Let me think about it." He was silent. "Max won't be joining us?"

"No. But Luci will be coming with me."

"Luci," he repeated. "Actually, she was next on my list. She really is supposed to be before you, Sarah. You might say she led the way to you."

"I'm getting bored with this conversation. Do you agree or not?"

"Perhaps. I'll let you know tomorrow."

"It has to be tonight or not at all." She had to persuade him. "It's your best bet. You know I can't hold off Max for much longer."

"And you don't know if you want him involved." Ivan's tone was malicious. "I knew you'd react that way when I told you what

I was planning on doing to him when I got my chance. It was bound to torture you and set you in a panic. I know you so well, Sarah. Tell me, do you fuck him?"

"You really don't know me at all. The only thing Max and I share is the love of Luci and the desire to wipe you off the face of the earth."

"I think there's more than that. I can't tell you how that will add to my pleasure."

"Wouldn't it be strange if I actually managed to take you down before you got the chance to hurt any of my friends? Think about it. I put a bullet in you, and you haven't even touched me since that time in Santorini."

"I could have touched you." A hint of annoyance edged his voice. "It wasn't my choice."

"Then why are you hesitating now? I think you're lying."

He didn't speak for an instant, and Sarah sensed his rage. "I didn't want to hurry. I wanted at least a week with you. But I promise you I can make a day seem like a week. Come now, Sarah, come out and play with me."

Move quickly, don't let him change his mind. "Where?"

"I'll be outside the Seven Golden Caves."

It was done.

Sarah drew a deep, shaky breath as she hung up the phone. She felt exhausted. She hadn't been sure until the last minute that he'd agree to meet where she had a chance. Sarah would bet she could even function inside that cave better than Ivan.

"Luci, it's on. Go to the caves and get yourself set up," she whispered. From her backpack, she retrieved her Glock and an infrared detector.

March 1536

Calisto suppressed a deep sob, along with the desire to lie beside her Mitera and cry. Despite the terrible dagger cuts on her mother's legs, she couldn't give up now; she had to survive. She had to save them.

After inhaling a deep breath to clear the panic rising in her chest, she said, "You will walk, Mitera. We have the mykite to heal your wounds."

Mitera's hand shot out and cupped Calisto's cheek. "My love, always the strong one with so much faith."

"I learned everything I know from you." She glanced over her shoulder again. The tangle of burnt rope was almost off her wrists. "Hurry, Mitera, please hurry."

Her Mitera picked for a few more minutes, and the last strand broke, freeing Calisto's burnt arms. She stared at what would become a scarred mess. Calisto swallowed hard and pushed back the tears that threatened to pour from her eyes.

Calisto was filled with renewed determination. Never would she live in bounds. Never would she assign limits to the desires to which she'd always strived. No, she would survive.

Calisto joined her Mitera, picking the ropes at her ankles. She ignored her raw fingers and the horrific smell. Every movement shot flashes of torment up her arms. After a few minutes, they finally got her legs free.

"Wait, Mitera. Let me look outside."

Calisto jumped up and raced to the door. Cautiously, she pulled it open with her burnt fingertips and peered out. The young warrior was nowhere around. Just then, the sun burst over the hills in an orange fireball, lighting the garden. Calisto stepped out and raced around the house. Everything was as it should be. In the early dawn, the birds chirped and flapped in the trees while the animals pawed in impatience for their food.

Today she could not attend to their needs.

Calisto ran back inside. With careful, precise movements to avoid knocking her wounded hands, she lifted out the clay pots that had her drawings and notes on mykite.

Flinching in pain, she grabbed the pot and placed it in her bag. Everything she touched scraped her raw skin. It all had to be ignored.

Calisto knelt beside her mother. "Mitera, let's go quickly."

"Calisto, take the pot and hide it in the cavern. Then come back for me."

"No, Mitera, I'm not leaving you here alone. The warriors will be back in minutes to hurt us."

"But, Calisto!"

"Mitera! We will never surrender. Better to die than to give up."

March 29, 2020

"Sarah, are you sure you remember a place in the cave for me to hide? He really has a thing for torture and death."

"Yes, but this isn't going to be simple. How do you intend to do it?"

"He wants me. But he doesn't want me dead. At least not at first. I'm counting on using that." She showed Luci the infrared detector. And I may be able to find him before he finds you or me."

"I've seen that gadget. You used it once before when we were looking for the lost document at Montsegur. It was handy."

"Yes, it was."

"So, you intend to track Ivan?"

"Yes, but it may end up with letting him track us. You know he'll know when you enter those caves. I'll just make sure I lose him right away so that I have a chance once he pounces." She turned to Luci. "How long until we get there?"

"I think another twenty minutes, give or take."

"Go into the grotto and wait for me at least five minutes." Her hands were moist with sweat as she clutched the duffel bag holding the guns.

He was coming closer. Ivan was coming closer.

Luci took Sarah's hand. "We're going to be okay, Sarah, I know it."

"Yes." Her hand tightened on Luci's. She couldn't be afraid. This was the moment she had been waiting for.

Ivan...

***

"Nick, where's Sarah and Luci?" Max asked.

"I thought they were back with Calisto's guards," Nick said.

"Do you think they'd go after Ivan alone?"

"I hope not, but if they do, I still have a tracker in Sarah's duffel bag."

"Thank God. Let's go."

***

She's coming, I can feel it. He peered into the shadowy darkness of the first of the seven caves. Yes, these caves were all full of shadows. Ivan had cast that giant shadow, and the fools didn't even realize it. He was always ahead of Max and company. The thought made him feel close to Sergei. Not that he wouldn't cast an even greater shadow when he took the gold and mykite from the caves.

***

Katerina caught up with Sarah and Luci as they reached the caves. "I'm going with you."

"No, you're not," Luci said. "You have to take care of your people."

"I know the caves better than you. I can be of help, and I will avenge my mother."

Luci hesitated. "I don't like this one bit." She turned back toward the cave. "Stay with me. Be careful, Sarah."

She didn't watch Sarah leave to hide but glided quickly into the forest. "Come on, Katerina. Stay close."

"Oh, I will, I promise."

***

Sarah stopped as she reached the shelter outside the first cave. She could almost hear her grandfather. *Listen. Watch the bushes for any movement.*

Was Ivan close?

She took out her infrared detector. Squirrels. Perhaps possums. No sign of any large life forms.

He's not anywhere near. I'll have to go deeper into the cave. She moved slowly forward.

Walk softly, her grandfather Louie had always told her. *Most animals have better hearing than we could possibly dream of having. Walk on the balls of your feet and watch the path to make sure you don't break a branch or even brush against the rocks.*

It all came back to her. She stood still again, using the detector to scan the darkness into the cave. Nothing close except small animals.

The guns…Sarah found a path winding snakelike through the cave. She placed the Glock beside one of the boulders and put rocks on top of it. She checked the Magnum she'd taken from Nick's suitcase. She was surprised that Ivan hadn't made his move yet. She was expecting—

A shot shattered the silence!

Sarah dropped to her knees before she realized that the shot had come from behind her—from the direction Luci and Katerina had gone. Someone was with Ivan, but who?

Only one shot. Luci or Katerina?

Sarah looked back, she was tense and concerned. She wanted to go to them, help them. But she couldn't.

Sarah hurried through the cave, hoping that Luci had turned back and was heading out to get Max and Nick. There was danger all around them, but Ivan was her threat, and Sarah had a gut instinct that he was coming for her now.

Keep safe, my friend.

She was a hundred yards deeper into the cave, but there was still no sign of Ivan. Was he there, watching her, letting her come closer before he pounced?

No, she trusted her instincts. She would have heard him, sensed him.

Another fifty yards and she used the detector again.

She stiffened. That was no small animal. It was a single large figure straight ahead.

She drew her gun and inched forward.

"Are you there, Sarah?" Ivan called. "I can't hear you, but I can feel you. I'll always be able to sense you near me. When two people are as close as we are, that's the way it will always be."

She froze. Was he taking a wild gamble, or did he really know?

"I'll give you two minutes to give up, then I'll spray this entire cave with bullets. I have my AK-47. It will take you down before you can get near me."

AK-47. Yes, she'd seen what that weapon could do. He may be lying, but he carried one frequently when he moved around the compound. A handgun would be worse than useless against it. She had known he might do something to weigh the odds to his side.

Unless she could take him by surprise.

And she had already set the surprise in motion when she hid the Glock by the boulder.

"One minute," Ivan called. "I don't want to cut you in two with those bullets, Sarah. It's so messy and entirely unsatisfying."

She moved quickly toward the sound of his voice.

"Sarah."

She stopped. "I'm on the path."

"Good, you're smart. Stay where you are. I'm going to take a look before I come out in the open. I want to make sure you're not too smart."

She stood, staring straight ahead. She felt him looking at her. He was right...that repulsive closeness was like a bond linking them.

"Hello, Sarah." Ivan strolled out from behind a large boulder cradling the AK-47 in his arm. There was a thick bandage on his right shoulder, but it didn't seem to hinder him. "Now stand very still while I search you. You have a weapon, I'm sure of it."

"Of course I do." She stood still, gritting her teeth as his hands slowly moved over her. Stopping on her breasts. He proceeded down and found the gun in her jacket, and stepped back. "How else could I hope to kill you?"

He chuckled. "But it's not doing you any good, is it? Now, where is your sister? Sergei saw Luci enter the forest with you. I'm not really worried that she may leap out and attack me. She's one of those do-gooders who will always be a victim."

"When we heard the shot, she went back to see if she could be of help to any of the people of Helike."

"Too late for any of them. There won't be anyone left alive to help. Sergei will see to that. All that will be left is for her to pray over their bodies." His lips curled viciously. "Stupid bitch."

"She's not stupid." She studied his expression. "And I don't believe you think she is. But you're angry with her. Why would a do-gooder manage to upset you so much?"

"She doesn't upset me. Enough. If I'd had time, I'd have—" He stopped. "But I will have time if Sergei doesn't kill her. I'll have you both. It was kind of you to bring her with you. Of course, I'm disappointed you didn't bring Max. I didn't think you'd pull him into this. Though he might come calling anyway. He appears to be quite devoted to Luci and you."

"You killed his friend."

"That's true. He was tough to break. He's going to be very pissed off that I took you and Luci away from him. I half expect him to come swooping down to the rescue. Just like your Superman." He smiled. "But you chose not to bring in the big guns. I knew you wouldn't. That's why I took the opportunity when you offered it. It was too good a chance to pass up. I can always get Max and Nick later. You'll make excellent bait to lure them out."

Bait. Yes, Max would come after her. He probably was trying to find them right now. The idea sent panic racing through her body. She had to get this over before he found a way to do it.

***

"The blip on the monitor has stopped," Nick said. "Sarah must have stopped moving."

"How far?" Max asked.

"Just a few miles to the southwest." He frowned. "It could be—"

"What?" Max asked.

"I'm not certain. But she's walking toward one of the seven caves."

***

"Why here, Ivan?" Sarah asked, her gaze going to the looming darkness. "Are you playing a mind game on me?"

"Yes, I do like mind games, but no, in this case, I want to be able to see who's coming after you. Then I can shoot them."

Sarah shuddered, wondering where Luci was hidden.

"We're going together to locate the gold in the seven caves, and we're going to find the magical secrets. You know what it is, and I want it."

"You're sick, I'll never tell you what's written inside the caves. Actually, I don't even know. I'm not an expert in that area."

"Yes, but Luci is. You're close, aren't you, Luci? Waiting, watching for your opportunity to kill me. I'm going to enjoy our time together, Sarah—and Luci can watch it. We're going to enjoy these last moments together, the three of us." His finger reached out and touched her cheek. "So brave, and yet so foolish."

"You're right, Luci is here, but you'll be dead before you can touch me again."

His finger remained on her cheek. "You might as well have come alone. Max, Nick, and Luci will be nothing for me to get rid of. Sergei has probably taken one of them down already."

"I'm surprised you have someone as loyal to you as Sergei. He has the same killer instincts, doesn't he?"

"Yes, he's been useful. I'll be sorry to have to dispose of him when this is over."

"Even Sergei?"

"He's a witness. I kept as much as I could from him, but he still knows far too much. But I don't want to talk about him. He'll do his job. I'm too absorbed with you, my dear Sarah."

This sent a chill through her body.

***

Luci heard everything Ivan was saying to Sarah, and had yet to figure out how to shoot him without the bullets flying all over the cave and maybe hitting Sarah or possibly herself.

The sound of a footstep shuffled very close behind her. Luci spun around. Sergei stood there, listening to everything that Ivan had just admitted.

She opened her mouth to say something. Sergei looked down at her and signaled to keep quiet.

***

"And you're infatuated with me," Ivan said softly. "I can feel your fear. It's making me hard. I don't really like to fuck women, but you've always been the exception. Back at the compound when I had finished with Max's friend for the day, I would come in and sit beside you, watch you. It was the most exquisite sexual thrill I'd ever known. You've become quite the obsession to me."

Her stomach churned. "Take your hand off of me."

"Soon." His head bent, and his lips hovered over hers.

"Do you know what I'll do if you bite me this time? I've thought of many new things I could do to Max that I never tried on Max's friend."

His tongue licked at her lower lip. "Then bite me, Sarah. Sink your teeth into me and show me that—"

Another shot rang out.

Sarah jerked away, her gaze flying in the direction from where the sound had come. Behind the boulder, she spotted Sergei holding an AK-47.

Sarah bent over to where Ivan lay. "I have to be sure." She turned him over. Blood bubbled from a wound in his chest, and a faint line trickled from the side of his mouth. At first, she thought he was dead, but he slowly opened his eyes.

"Sarah..." Then, incredibly he smiled. "I'm not going to die. I'll heal and come back, and I'll do whatever...I want with you."

"You're dying now, Ivan. You probably have only a few more moments to live."

Sergei and Luci came out from behind the boulder, Sergei holding onto Luci's arm. "If I thought you'd live, Ivan, I'd put another bullet in you," Sergei said.

"No, I'm going to—" He screamed in agony and slumped over. He was dead.

***

Max and Nick came through the cave, guns were drawn. "Put your gun down, Sergei."

Sergei's gun clattered to the rocky cave floor.

Luci ran to Max. "You shouldn't have been here," he said to Luci and Sarah.

"No, you're wrong," Sarah said. "I had the right to be here. It's over now. I can breathe again."

"Sarah, you're bleeding. Are you hurt?" Nick asked, concern in his eyes.

"It's just scrapes from the rocks. I'll be fine, Nick."

Luci and Max looked at Sarah and Nick noticing that Sergei had sneaked out of the cave.

Suddenly a piercing scream made them all alert.

March 1536

Once again, Calisto knelt beside her Mitera and placed a hand under her back in an attempt to lift her. A searing shudder of pain shot through Calisto's body, tipping her forward. She stumbled and righted herself. Breathing deeply, she tried again.

Although she was far from the fire, it felt as if the flames still licked at her arms. Under the skin, they played with her flesh, making it feel as if her arms were buried in the heat. Calisto grunted and gritted her teeth to stop herself from flinching. She didn't want her Mitera to witness her pain.

"It's no use." Mitera tried to sit up but instead leaned to her left, like a tree falling in a storm. "Calisto, we must heal your hands before you can carry me."

Calisto tried again to lift her Mitera but cried out as a blistered layer of skin came off one of her arms. The smell of her burnt flesh was still so thick and rich she could taste it.

"Stop it! Calisto! Listen to me."

Startled, Calisto stopped what she was doing and stared at her Mitera.

"You are wasting precious time. Go get some mykite. We need to heal your hands, and then you can help me."

"But Mitera, what if they come back? They will murder you and come after me." Calisto stood her ground. "I will not ever leave you."

"Calisto, you are so stubborn. Please go fetch your Patera's tool bag."

"What are you going to do, Mitera?"

Had Mitera had the same thought as she? No, she did not have an evil bone in her body.

Gently laying her Mitera on the floor, she mumbled, "I will get his bag."

Mitera frowned at her. "I see that mischievous look in your face. What are you up to?"

Calisto bent down and kissed her Mitera's forehead. "Everything will work out, I promise."

Knowing the young warrior would not be far from the house, Calisto peered out then leaped across the cobblestones. When she reached her Patera's workshop, she stopped and glanced down the path, half expecting to see an Incan warrior.

She had to hurry; he would be back at any moment.

Calisto ran to the tool shed. With throbbing fingertips, she picked a long chisel with the thinnest, most pointed shaft, and Patera's stonemason's hammer. It had a flat surface with a long chisel-shaped blade. Many a time she had watched her Patera use it to chip off small pieces of stone.

Armed with Patera's tools, she raced to the kitchen. Her mother still lay on the floor but strained to move.

"Mitera, lay down, please."

"Did you get the stone?"

"What stone?" Calisto frowned. Mitera must be in so much pain she now spoke in riddles. "When the Incans return, we will pretend all is as they left."

"Why? You must escape before he—"

"Mitera, there is no time. Please just do as I say." Calisto slumped into her chair and coiled a piece of the shredded rope around her ankles. At that moment, heavy footsteps stomped up the cobblestones.

"Mitera, turn your head and don't look this way. I do not wish for you to see what I am about to do."

For once, Mitera listened to her daughter.

March 29, 2020

Nick, Luci, Max, and Sarah ran out of the cave toward the sound of the shot. They saw Katerina standing over the body of Sergei.

"Are you okay, Katerina?" Luci asked quietly.

"He was an evil man."

"Yes," Luci answered. "Sergei was a vile man." She wearily brushed the hair away from her face. "I'm glad you're okay, Katerina."

Sarah stopped on the path and looked back at Sergei. The moonlight was full on his face, and that last, enraged, incredulous expression was frozen in time—his eyes wide open staring up at the sky.

"Sarah?"

"Even now, I feel he could stand up and hurt us all."

"But he can't, he's dead. He can't hurt anyone else again." Luci turned her back on Sergei and grasped Max's arm. "Let's go back to the temple and figure out our next steps."

March 1536

Calisto held her hands behind her back, one armed with the chisel and the other with the hammer. She slowed her breathing. Whatever happened, she must not alert the Incan.

The young warrior kicked the door open and marched to her side. He reeked of sweat while his boots sent a damp, earthy smell up Calisto's nose.

"Where is the well?" he screamed in her face, spitting his foul breath on her cheeks. "You're a liar."

Calisto waited. Her head hung low over her pounding chest.

He leaned over and yanked back her thick hair. Calisto launched herself into the air, both arms thrusting up. She lunged the chisel into the Incan's chest and slammed the hammer over his head.

He fell against her, gripping his chest and crying out in anguish. You're a Tlahulpuchi!"

As the sunlight burst into the window blinding her, a fuse kindled inside Calisto. Without thinking, she shoved the warrior off her and clubbed him again with the hammer. Hundreds of tiny sparks of pain shot through her hands, but Calisto ignored them. She had only their escape to think about.

One last feeble groan spilled from the Incan's lips as he fell on the floor beside Mitera. Calisto bent over him. A stream of dark blood oozed out of his head. He was dead.

Calisto turned to her mother. "Mitera! We must leave. Now!"

Mitera nodded and lifted her arms. She didn't look at the warrior.

Calisto helped her Mitera use every ounce of her strength to haul herself to her knees. "Here, grab hold of me. Lean on my back, so I can keep my hands free."

Mitera nodded and lifted her arms. Calisto and Matera spent the next few minutes grunting and groaning as they got into a comfortable position to escape from their home. Keeping her hands free, Calisto used her elbow and hips to shunt her Mitera into place. She insisted her mother lean on her so she could drag her.

"Calisto, wait. You must get Patera's stone."

Calisto ignored her Mitera's pleas. "Please, Mitera, it's dangerous, the other warriors will surely arrive here soon."

Before they had taken one step, Calisto realized it would take hours, maybe days, to get to the caves. It was usually a short walk, but with her burnt hands and Mitera's tattered legs, they would be lucky to get to safety before the men returned.

"Here, Mitera, hang on me. I will drag you, like a horse dragging a load."

"I'm burdening you, you should go on without me."

"We will mend you in the caves, Mitera. That is what you would do for me. You put our people back in order when their bodies have come apart. You have taken care of any ailment you have met as an adversary. Now we will do the same for you."

Mitera smiled and took one last look around her kitchen.

Determined to get off, Calisto stepped forward with her Mitera hanging from her shoulders like a rag doll. "Let's go."

March 29, 2020

They walked back to the temple, where Max pulled Luci away from the rest of the group. Luci turned to him and braced herself. "I don't want you to come with me once we leave the temple."

"So, is this a goodbye?" His lips twisted. "You're cutting me loose after all we've been through."

"I need to wipe the slate clean. I don't want uncertainty coming from either side." She paused. "I want to put time and space between us. I want to know that it wasn't a circumstance or pity that brought us back together again."

"I don't pity you, Luci. For God's sake, you should know that by—" He stopped. "I'm not going to change your mind, am I?"

"Time and space, Max," she repeated. She would not cry. She was right. This was best for both of them.

But it hurt so much.

"Then get the hell out of here. Start chalking up your damn time. Because I'm going to be on your doorstep before you know it. Be ready for me, Luci."

She'd be ready for him. She was ready now.

March 1536

Mitera took a step and cried in pain. She stumbled to the ground dragging Calisto with her. "I can't make it."

"We will. Please, Mitera, we'll go slowly, one step at a time."

"Why are you so stubborn? For once, listen to your Mitera. I think it is better if you fetch the mykite to heal your hands and then bring some back to heal me."

"Mitera, we can't risk it. Can we go now?"

Mitera flinched but nodded.

Calisto took a step. It took nearly an hour to get out of the door.

Dragging her Mitera over the croft proved to be the worst part of the journey. They tripped over each cobblestone. A few times, Mitera's arms came loose. Each time, Calisto knelt on the stones and shuffled her body under her mother's.

Mitera had little strength left. If only she could use her hands. Calisto wouldn't be able to carry her Mitera; she was far too heavy. But at least she was able to drag her along, however slowly.

In the distance, Calisto heard the sound of men coming. The warriors were back!

Calisto and her mother stood frozen in their tracks. They listened to the laughing in the distance, expecting them to come closer. After a few moments, the sound disappeared.

"We must hurry, Mitera."

"The warriors are everywhere, Calisto. You must leave me. There's still time."

"Quiet, Mitera. I won't let them have you."

"Calisto, I have an idea. Leave me in our cellar. They will never find me there locked under the ground. You go…get the mykite. Then come back for me."

Calisto tried to interrupt, but Mitera poked her back.

"When you see they are not here, open the cellar door. There is food enough for…many days. We can hide until we are both strong enough to escape."

"But Mitera—"

"This is the only way, Calisto. Can you not see, your stubbornness will get us both killed?"

Mitera's crying made Calisto squirm. If she could get her hands even a little better, she would be of more use to them both. "I will go, Mitera, and I will be right back."

Calisto used her remaining strength to drag her mother to the cellar. After she lifted the hidden wooden lid, she gritted her teeth against the agony of going downstairs. A sense of accomplishment spurred her on, even though the smell of her burning flesh would not leave her.

With one last glance back at her mother, Calisto exited the cellar. She placed a few twigs and a layer of green branches over the wooden lid. Covered in animal feed, it looked part of the stable floor.

The animals cried out to be fed. Her heart skipped a beat. Getting help for Mitera came first.

Even if her hands were able to feed the animals, the returning soldiers would know she had been strong enough to escape. They would ransack the farm in their search, and they might find the cellar where her poor Mitera lay.

Calisto had to get to the cavern first.

The cave's secret held their only hope.

***

Calisto entered the close cropping of trees that surrounded the grotto. She waded across the shallow pond where the mykite grew on the rocks.

Before collecting the slimy golden mushrooms, she had one more task to carry out. High above, a dark black hole scarred the rocky outcrop that hid a secret.

Usually scaling up, she only reached here and there for support. Today, she reached out every few steps. The horror of the past day made her weak and helpless. The pain in her hands sapped the last threads of strength she had left.

At the entrance of the cave, Calisto rested for a moment to catch her breath. Whenever she came to collect the mykite and explore the caves, she passed the sharp rocks along the walls and ceiling. Yet now, the tunnel leading into the hidden cave looked as though it showed its jagged teeth, like a jaguar forbidding anyone to enter.

Normally, the damp sour smell of earth didn't trouble her, but today it made her sick.

With a ceiling three times the height of her home, she could look out at the golden pond below. Beyond, the wooded forest kept the caves hidden. Inside, at one end of the cave, water plunged into a vast pool. Here, Calisto could dive into water that shone as blue as the sky.

In the middle, the cave's rook opened up, like clouds parting to let the sun through. On the far side, the pool descended into another lower cave in the depths of the earth.

Climbing deeper into the back of the cave, Calisto searched for her hiding place. On some rocks, skinny figures brandishing staffs and spears followed the stars to their new homeland. The yellow ochre star leaped high in the sky. Calisto spotted her beloved painting on the rock and went straight to it.

The usual hiding place for her secrets.

***

Her Mitera had described the long voyage across the seas and escaping the Incans. One of her paintings was of arrows raining down on the Helikes as they ran for the volcano. When she had run her fingers along a drawing she had made of her father, his powerful chest, and her beautiful mother, she had discovered an empty alcove.

Since then, she had used it as a hiding place to keep secrets, even Mitera did not know. "Take care of my codex," she whispered.

With careful movements, Calisto squeezed the cylinder into the hole. For now, the mykite would be safe beside the drawing of her parents. One day, she would return, but now, it was too dangerous to keep.

Turning back, she glanced at the rock wall. Her father stood proud, his head turned slightly as if he watched her every move.

Back beside the cave's pond, Calisto slumped and used her burnt fingertips to pluck the mushrooms off the rocks. The only way to crush the curly, golden fungi was between her hands. The rubbing made them bleed again. Biting hard on a twig, Calisto ground the mykite into her wounds. Spasms of agony clawed up her arms. Within seconds, her whole body trembled. Her breathing leaped around in her chest like a frog chasing a bug.

When she could take no more, Calisto fell back against the damp grass and shrieked in pain. "Why, God, why?"

Biting down on the twig once more, Calisto ground another batch of sticky mykite. In slow motion, she smeared the slimy golden paste across her hands and up her arms.

The odor of her mother's dirty hair blended with her own burnt flesh still clung to her nose. Calisto dropped her face into the water and shook her nose around to rid herself of the horrible smell, lest it sickened her even more.

As Calisto sat beside the pond, she remembered the day it started, the day she had rescued the wounded Incan boy.

Now, for the first time, she noticed how the water was thicker with slime at the edges beside the rocks where the mushroom grew. She trailed her palms across the surface. The cool water licked at the sticky paste, giving instant relief. The heat inside her skin cooled, so she spent a few more minutes stroking the water. As she did so, she wondered if the water increased the healing powers of the mykite. It felt that way.

The cave's peaceful tranquility relaxed Calisto. The heat of the midday sun gave everything around her a chance to rest. She lay back on the grassy bank with her hands hanging in the water, her mind drifting and her eyes closing.

Calisto woke with a start. She sat up and peered around her. The sun headed towards the horizon. "Oh no! I have to get back to Mitera!"

She leaped to her feet, angry.

Something else caught her eye.

Smoke rose into the sky from the direction of her home!

***

Calisto raced home. Her mouth dropped open as she gazed at the destruction. The animals were scattered about her mother's garden, grazing. Mitera's pots and pans littered the cobblestones around the house. The warriors had left but destroyed her home.

Calisto called out. "*Mitera!*"

Only then did she discover the worst. In their anger, the Incans had set the donkey stable alight. The blaze had twisted the stone pillars from their foundations, crushing the roof on top of the cellar.

Calisto dropped to her knees to lift the smoldering thatched roof. The weight of it and the stone from the walls was too much for her. Even if her hands weren't recovering, she would never be able to get into the cellar.

"Mitera, Mitera!" Calisto ran around the shed and tried to crawl between the pieces of rubble. No space was substantial enough to creep into. How could she get into the cellar to rescue her mother? She couldn't even see the wooden door under the pile of burnt wood and blackened stones.

The destroyed stable wouldn't have harmed her hidden under the ground. Mitera should be safe.

"*Mitera, can you hear me?*" Calisto lay flat against the ground and listened for any sound. Maybe her mother was asleep. Calisto glanced over her shoulder, grimacing at her home burning to the ground.

Spotting a metal bucket amongst the broken stone, she raced to grab it and ran to the water barrel. She sank the bucket inside and threw water over the flames at the back of the house. It wouldn't save their home, but she tried anyway. Calisto spent the next hour dousing the fire until the final drop of water had been used up.

Then, hoping Mitera would hear this time, Calisto ran to the rubble and called again. "Mitera."

She dug furiously. Each movement brought a fresh spurt of blood from her wounds. She could not lift the heavy wooden poles. In desperation, she raised her head and screamed, "*Mitera!*"

Still no answer.

***

Thunder cracked in the distance. Within seconds the darkening clouds opened, mourning with Calisto. Huge raindrops deadened the last of the flames eating away at her home. As thunder rolled across the sky, it revealed the truth Calisto couldn't face. Her Mitera had died of her wounds. Probably soon after Calisto left for the caves…she was too late.

Allowing the rain to wash away her grief, Calisto lay beside the cellar door. Overcome with guilt and despair, she wanted to close her eyes and never open them again.

How could she be so thoughtless falling asleep?

The lump in her throat ballooned, making it hard to swallow. Forgive me, Mitera, I'm so sorry!

Calisto lay still looking at the destruction and the ruins of the stable. She would rebuild the barn and pens for the poor animals, even her dear goat. Finally, bitterness and disappointment forced her to her feet. She paced around the farmyard, a jaguar searching for a way to keep intruders away from her people's valley forever. Calisto stopped to hold onto the lamb's head, then she stroked the head of the donkey.

Her father's workshop had been saved but had been ransacked. She stepped over the broken door and perched on the tree stump where Mitera had often sat to talk to Patera.

"Mitera, what do I do?"

Tears welled in her eyes again. She was alone in the world, her neighbors and friends scattered about in the forest. She would find them. They would rebuild the valley and build a great city like the one her people had once come from.

Calisto allowed her tears to flow freely. She sat on the wooden stump with her eyes closed. When she opened them, the tears had dried up. She dared not wipe her face while her hands were still healing and so she left the sticky tears on her skin.

For a long time, Calisto had longed to wear the Grecian gowns that her Mitera had owned but had given up for practical uses of building and gardening. She would find those gowns in her Mitera's trunk in the cellar.

Glancing around, she spotted one of Mitera's hair ribbons. She grabbed it and tied her hair as her mother had once done in the Grecian style.

The burst of rain finally stopped. The sky, too, had shed its tears. Dry-eyed, she prepared to leave. The Incans would come back. She wasn't about to let them.

***

Every part of Calisto wanted to run away, into the caves, but not now. The Incans knew who she was, and they would hunt her down. They might even ransack the village, thinking she would seek safety there.

She wished the sun would appear and lift her spirits. Instead, a peaceful yet plaintive call wafted towards her. Strange tranquility descended and drew her outside, carrying her father's tool bag and black powder. She glanced at Mitera's bakehouse and ambled toward it. Its door was broken down. The warriors had found nothing inside but baking tools. Mitera had used the bakehouse to hang the wild game neighbors had brought her in payment for her healing potions. Testing the use of her fingertips, Calisto lifted a pan and dusted it off.

"Your favorite pan, Mitera." She had no idea why she spoke aloud, but hearing the words comforted her, as though Mitera was still there, listening, advising her. Placing it in the back of the stone oven, she said, "I loved the bread you made with the herbs you harvested outside."

Calisto cleared the bakehouse wishing she could fix the door. Stepping outside, she shook her head at the trampled herb garden. She hoped Mitera's herbal secrets were safe in the cellar. She felt a bitter twinge of irony that her mother's precious herbs would die with her.

"Never mind, Mitera, I will draw in my daybook about your herbs. You always said I had a good memory."

Talking to Mitera eased the emptiness in her heart, but she had to leave. Mitera had insisted that she escape so she could live. She would do that and make her Mitera proud.

As she crossed the forest, Calisto glanced at her home; the rain-soaked beams still hissed, and the thatch roof still smoldered with acrid smoke. With the smell of death and destruction wafting around the farm, Calisto knew what she must do.

***

Calisto gathered the surrounding villagers. Her Mitera had helped and enlisted them in her plan to destroy the only entrance to the valley.

Steadily they walked together. The men took her father's tool bag with the black powder she had seen him use to remove trees or outcroppings of boulders so the animals would have room to roam and grass for feed.

Calisto and the villagers made their way through the valley floor to the caves where an opening had been created with the last volcano eruption. Placing the gunpowder around the boulders, they dropped the powder as they made their way out of the grotto.

A man had flint and struck the powder. It lighted and soon made its way through the back of the caves, igniting the powder and sealing the outside world from the world Calisto was about to recreate with her friends and family from the island of Helike.

She would go back home to build a temple in commemoration for her people to live, work, and learn the old ways. Calisto would write down in her codex all the secret potions her Mitera had once used. She would replant the herb garden. On the way back, she spotted a small goat that had somehow escaped the fires. She gathered him in her arms, and with determination to begin anew, she and the villagers left the forest for their homes.

December, 2020

Monterey, California

Max walked down the beach toward Luci.

She stiffened, then forced herself to relax. Don't let it mean too much, she thought.

Bull. How could she help but let it mean too much? She had missed him every minute of every day since she had left him at the temple. Just seeing him smile threw her for a loop.

She stood up on the dune, her bare feet sinking into the warm sand as she faced him. "You're looking...well."

"Is that all you've got to say?" he asked. "I've been waiting for you to call me for almost a year. I was wondering if you'd ever get around to it."

"It took a long time for the media to go away." She paused. "And I wanted to make sure that all the scars were on the way to healing. We learned so much from Calisto. I really miss her. I wasn't going to be good for anyone until I was good for myself."

"You had to do that alone?" His face was without expression. "You had to close me out?"

"I thought I did."

And she hadn't been sure he would tolerate her. She still wasn't sure. He had come when she called, but now that he was here, she couldn't read him. She turned and stared down the dune. "Will you walk me back to my condo?"

"Why not?" He fell into step beside her. "It's the first thing you've asked of me. I had to watch you go through that hell and all the media attention, and I couldn't do a thing to help you."

"It wasn't pleasant, but it wasn't hell. I just had to hold on to the knowledge that it too would pass." She smiled faintly. "I'm going back to work soon. I've got my head together now and know where I'm going."

"Which is?"

"I'll be working with Sarah and Nick and the archeological company. We have a new project in Syria."

"Look, I don't care about that," he spat, roughly. And I'm tired of your talking about anything other than us. I want you to talk about me. I want you to talk about us. That's why I came here. Now cut to the chase. You've had your time and space. A hell of a lot too much of both for me. Now talk to me."

"What do you want me to say, Max?" No, that was too passive, and she was not feeling the least passive. "And just why did you come here? It could be because you wanted to tell me that I was right to take that time, and you decided that we couldn't make a relationship work because we live in two different places and serve different masters. How do I know?"

She stepped closer.

"But here's what I do know. I've never met a man I wanted as much as I do you. Do I love you? I think I do, but I'm never going to be sure unless I live with you and share something besides threats and trauma. We deserve that chance to discover who we really are together. So that's what I'm going to do. If you don't want to do that, then I'll just have to follow you around and dog you everywhere you go. You'll have to have me arrested as a stalker to get rid of me. And when they let me out of jail, I'll come to you again." She drew a deep breath. "So why not save time and give in now? I promise I'll make it worth your while."

He smiled. "What an interesting offer."

"Is that all you've got to say?"

"Yes, I'd better accede graciously because I'm clearly not going to change your mind." He cupped her face in his hands and said thickly, "Thank God."

For a moment, she couldn't get her breath for the rush of sheer joy. "Oh, yes, thank God," she said unsteadily. "I believe that means I'm not going to have to do any serious pursuing."

He kissed her lightly. "It means that I'm taking you up on your promise to make it worth my while." He kissed her again, not so gently. "For the next fifty or sixty years. After that, we'll renegotiate." He pushed her away and took her hand. But right now, you're going to show me your condo. It does have a bed, right?"

"Oh, yes."

"Then we'll start there, and who knows we may end up back there again." He smiled down at her. His warm hand grasped hers as they started down the path through the woods. "If we're embarking on this journey of discovery, I think I want to know more of you."

***

@lucidefoix u won this one dear Luci, but I'll be waiting for you

Separating Fact from Fiction

- Mykite: South America has a jungle that many scientists believe hide a treasure trove of medical cures for all humanity. Sadly, mykite is from my imagination.
- There are thousands of unexplored areas in South America that could have lost gold and temples. The Incans were said to have hidden their gold away from Pizarro and other intruders.
- There have been many adventurers and scientists who have explored South America and who have never been heard from again or were found murdered.

Thank you

I just wanted to take a moment to say thank you for choosing to spend your time reading my work. I am honored and hope you enjoyed it.